THE
PLACE
BEYOND
HER
DREAMS

THE
PLACE
BEYOND
HER
DREAMS

OBY ALIGWEKWE

ECLAT BOOKS

This book is a work of fiction. Characters, names, and events as well as all places, incidents, organizations, and dialog in this novel are either the products of the writer's imagination or are used fictitiously – not portrayed with geographical and historical accuracy.

Cover design by Stefanie Saw
Author photo by Mina Dacosta

Visit: www.obyaligwekwe.com

For Dumkelechi and Nnamdi

"The two most important days in your life are the day you are **born** and the day you find out **why.**"

-Mark Twain-

CHAPTER ONE

I HAD JUST turned ten the day Okem came to live with us. Everything was positioned as it had been every Saturday since I moved in with my grandparents. My grandmother was in the study tinkering with her sewing machine, I was at her feet hemming a sleeve, and my grandfather was entertaining visitors in the sitting room.

Startled by a burst of laughter from my grandfather, I dashed to the sitting room, which was separated by a narrow hallway from the study. His body vibrated. He slapped his knees with such intensity he'd failed to see me standing next to him. Turning to look in my direction after he noticed his visitors—a man and a woman—staring at me, he hurriedly beckoned to me.

That gesture—my grandfather ushering me into

his magnificent presence and allowing me to sit on the softly cushioned chair next to his—used to be the highlight of my days. I moved forward to settle beside him, and right before my back hit the chair, I discovered the source of his amusement. The boy. A mere boy, standing in the corner, holding a straw fan.

"Repeat," my grandfather said, pointing and waving his index finger at the boy.

The scraggly boy performed a contorted dance, twisting his body and strumming his fingers against the fan, pretending it was a guitar.

"Wasn't that funny?" my grandfather asked, chuckling and looking down at me.

"It's funny, Papa," I agreed, trying to suppress a giggle.

"Have you greeted our guests?" my grandfather's voice boomed in my ears—a reminder to comport myself accordingly.

"Good evening, Sir. Good evening, Ma'am," I said, bowing my head slightly.

"Good evening, little one," the woman responded.

I placed both hands on the chair, crossed my legs, and scrutinized the couple. The woman, with her oval face and full pouty lips, seemed well-mannered, though she spoke strangely. I recalled where I'd heard the dialect and cringed. She was from Ide, a town embroiled in boundary clashes with Ntebe, my picturesque hillside town. It was then I realized my grandfather had not been settling a domestic dispute, which made the strangers a little more interesting to me. He also couldn't have been addressing a boundary issue with Ide, as I was never allowed near him when the chiefs met to discuss boundaries. He always said it was strictly for adults.

The man sitting next to the woman—Ozumba, they called him—appeared jittery, constantly scratching his balding head. He avoided looking at me, but I couldn't fathom why. Perhaps he wanted me to leave. He tugged at the sleeves of his matching embroidered brocade outfit, which seemed a little too tight on him.

* * *

As my mind went around in circles pondering the purpose of their visit, as I'd become accustomed to, I caught a glimpse of the future—a small flash of Okem's face staring intently at me. Before I could make any sense of what I'd seen, and figure out if it was good, bad, or completely inconsequential, my grandfather called me back to earth. Okem had taken the seat next to the couple and proceeded to watch me. I followed his gaze and noticed he'd been admiring the sparkly red shoes my grandfather got me the last time he visited London. "Dorothy's shoes," Papa had called them. They reminded him of the ruby slippers from *The Wizard of Oz*.

"Hello," I said, grinning and waving my hand

slowly when Okem looked up and gave me a faint smile.

"Hi," he responded, leaning uncomfortably into his seat and locking his ankles.

One look at his clothes told me he was of a lower status. His intonation didn't help matters. Before I got the chance to complete my assessment, my grandfather announced, "It's concluded. Okem will stay with us. We'll take care of him like our own. There's no need to worry. He'll go to school with all the other kids in the town, and in the future, he may even become a doctor and make you proud."

Hearing my grandfather tell total strangers that their son would come to our house and distort the dynamics I'd only just become accustomed to, created the tightest feeling in the pit of my stomach. I remember wondering why my grandfather had not forewarned me.

Right then, I heard my grandmother calling.

"Ona...Ona."

I excused myself and left the room. After a few steps, the image I'd seen earlier came back to me.

"Grandma," I called, taking a second to stare at her delicately aging face. I admired the way the wrinkles formed a crescent around her mouth.

"Yes?" she answered, raising her brows.

"Do you approve of that little boy coming to live with us?"

"Of course I do," she responded with a slight

chuckle. "Your grandfather and I discussed this some days ago. I didn't think you'd mind. We thought you'd be happy to have someone to play with after school. Consider him a gift from us, and you'll feel better about the whole situation. And he's not a little boy. Okem is at least two years older than you."

"What?" I shrieked, mostly because she considered him a gift when in my mind, he was coming to steal their affection away from me.

"These people were kind enough to bring their boy to help around the house. In return, we'll make sure he's taken care of. He'll have a roof over his head, good food, and proper education. You'll be nice to him, won't you?"

"I'll try," I said with a humble sigh.

"Promise?"

Holding up my right hand, I agreed, not knowing what I was signing myself up for.

* * *

It didn't take long for Okem to adapt to our household. Every day, we walked to school together and played games after we came home. In the first couple of months, other kids whispered and made fun of his gaunt looks. My girlfriends joined in the bullying also. Okem hardly cared until one of the kids called him a "glorified house-boy." He fought the unfortunate child and ended up getting both of them bruised and disciplined in the process. I remember clearly when things slowly began to turn around. Amah, my best friend at the time, had come for a visit. Pointing at Okem's shoes, she'd said, "Is that from the second-hand store?" in the most condescending tone I'd ever heard.

My heart had skipped a beat. I wished Amah hadn't spoken, but she never let anything slide.

Before I could ask Okem to ignore her comment and focus on the dark clouds building up on the horizon, threatening heavy rain, he turned to Amah and responded calmly. "Were you speaking to me?"

Amah hissed, trembling slightly and looking over her shoulder.

That incident had forced me to start seeing Okem in a different light. He carried himself with a certain amount of pride and confidence that was odd for someone his age. Soon, the other kids noticed and began to accord him some respect.

* * *

I first moved in with my grandparents over a decade ago. My mother worked for a secret international government mission, and my father was the personal assistant to one of the top officials in the military. My parents traveled all the time, sometimes, for weeks on end. Living with them had been a security nightmare, or so my mother claimed. They were often targets for people who wanted access to the important officials they worked for. Growing up as an only child, since my parent's jobs didn't allow them to be in the same location most of the time, my grandfather convinced them to bring me to live with him and my grandmother.

My grandfather, or 'Papa' as I liked to call him, was a titled man—a chief. His usual attire, a red cap with three feathers stuck on one side, distinguished him from others. Men and women came into his presence daily to resolve all kinds of disputes, mostly domestic ones. I had always loved visiting my grandparents in their gorgeous country mansion in Ntebe. High ceilings, marble floors, polished stone pedestals bearing images of historical figures, and an orchard filled with mango trees and many varieties of oranges. What was there not to love? I couldn't remember a Christmas holiday I didn't spend with them, but when my mother told me I would leave my school and my friends—the ones I had played with for so many years—because I needed to move in with my grandparents, I sobbed for days. It didn't help that they had given me the news only two days before they shipped me off. A week before I traveled to my grandparents, I had woken up crying after one of those dreams that ended up being an account of a future I was soon to experience.

In my dream, I was an unaccompanied minor on board a Nigeria Airways flight. The pilot and the air hostesses had treated me nicely, making sure I had extra treats on the plane after they saw my swollen eyes—the aftermath of non-stop crying. My shipment to Ntebe had happened in the same way.

My grandparents, having heard about my misery, were distraught upon my arrival. I could hear my grandfather's heart shatter when he saw the pain in my eyes.

"*Ogini* Ona? What are you crying about?" he had asked.

I remember looking at him with tear-filled eyes. He had knelt before me, all six-foot-six of him, and covered my hand with his before raising my chin and staring at me with the kindest, most revealing eyes I'd ever seen—a moment I clearly remembered from my dream. At the time, I had thought his eyes were blue, but I later noticed the screen on the window that gave their brown shade a sapphire hue. He had winked at me as though he'd once shared that moment with me in another reality.

From that day onwards, my grandparents treated me like a princess. They gave me double my usual allowance and exempted me from chores, but only for one week as my grandmother didn't want me to be completely spoiled. Before long, I made friends at my new school and settled into a new existence. This new existence included Ifedi, my nanny, who my grandparents brought to live with us soon after I moved in. I liked Ifedi the moment I met her. She was older than me by at least ten years, but she was child-like. She braided my puffy hair in a new style every week, massaged my feet until I fell asleep, and ate my leftovers so my grandmother wouldn't scold me for wasting food. I liked her mostly because of the folktales she told me every night. I always assumed she concocted them to impress me, but I loved them anyway. Unlike the strict nanny I had when I lived with my parents, Ifedi brought so much excitement into my life.

My gift, or should I say my strange ability, to now and again catch glimpses of the future, was a welcome retreat at times. At other times, it presented an excruciating burden, so much so that I fought to force my brain to shut down to forget what I'd seen. Since my first experience at the age of seven, the uncertainty always caused me to stay on the edge in the other dimension and never really go inside to explore all it had to offer. It didn't matter if the revelations came through dreams, visions, or astral projection; I often faced the dilemma of trying to decide what predictions to share. Not everything I'd ever seen occurred, but many day-to-day occurrences ended up feeling like a déjà vu. My grandfather often caught me with that faraway look in my eyes. Intuition. That was his term for my gift. Several years later and uncountable trips into that realm, I now know just how far off his description was.

* * *

The love I had for my grandfather grew over the

months, and soon he could not do certain things without me. He would not eat his nightly meal if I wasn't by his side. Dinner was his favorite time for dishing out words of wisdom. He would ask Okem to bring an extra plate on which he would place pieces of fish and meat for me to munch on while I watched him eat. At intervals, he would look up from his plate and smile as I wiggled in my seat, giggling and telling stories about my day, stories that Ifedi had told me, or the things that had happened in school. My tales always amused him. One time, he almost choked as he laughed, and my grandmother came in with a horrible scowl on her face and demanded that I go to bed.

My grandfather had swiftly recovered when he heard her command.

"Leave her alone woman," he'd said, lifting the cup of palm wine in front of him and taking a gulp.

"She has school tomorrow. Look how late it is," my grandmother had countered.

"A few more minutes won't push her to the bottom of the class. Will it, Ona?" he'd asked, gently placing the cup on the table and looking at me for confirmation.

My grandfather was suave. I remember thinking that when I grew up, I would marry a man like him. Once, I had told him that. That must have been the happiest I'd ever seen him.

CHAPTER TWO

ONE MONTH AFTER my eleventh birthday, the desiccating north-east harmattan winds blew a flurry of red dust and some dirt as I walked into my grandfather's compound. I sprinted in the opposite direction as I feared the tornado would carry me away to some unknown land where I could never see my grandparents again. It subsided as quickly as it had started, but it left behind particles of dust and dirt, making it hard for me to see. I managed to observe the blockage caused by cars parked haphazardly on the road facing the compound and extending into our driveway. It then made sense why my school bus driver had asked me to alight a block from my home. I was not happy about the fact that I had to walk. The dust had turned my white stockings a reddish-brown, which meant I wouldn't receive my usual compliments from my grandfather, who often marveled at how my clothes always remained so clean even after a full day at school. Every day, I removed my stockings during the break period and put them back on after I had played with my friends—that's how important their cleanliness, and my grandfather's praise, was to me.

I got closer to the gate and discovered there were more important things to contend with than my stockings. A throng of visitors was inside the compound, some seated on benches, others leaning on their cars, and several more whispering in little circles. No one had noticed when I walked in. I felt invisible and remained so as I crept by the men and women that blocked the entrance to the staircase and every single stair, all the way to the landing.

I pushed and shoved countless times until I finally made it past the hallway that led to my grandmother's private parlor. Stopping for a moment to catch my breath, I started to hear crying; something had gone seriously wrong. Not crying from just one or two people, but enough people to create an orchestra of moaning and wailing that grew louder as I drew closer. I placed my forehead against the frosted glass partition that separated the room from the hallway and noticed a swarm of people looking down. The door refused to give when I turned the knob, so I banged as hard as I could before someone hurriedly opened it.

"Oh, dear. Look who it is," one of the visitors said.

The moaning suddenly stopped as everyone, except for my grandmother, turned to look in my direction. She kept her head down.

I was now certain something terrible had happened. My grandmother, my usually composed and immovable Grandma was sitting on her couch, flanked by two women, their hands interlocked as though the whole order of the universe would be disrupted if they let go of one another. Her chest heaved wildly as she took in air in large gasps. Someone whispered something into her ear, causing her head to shoot up. I recoiled in horror when I saw her eyes, startled by the stark red taking over the whites, as red as the harmattan dust I had just left behind. She squinted to look at me and then let out a loud wail as she rested both hands on her head. I ran to her side, and she wrapped her hands so tightly around me, I thought I would suffocate.

"We're done for," she sobbed, shaking her head wildly and staring at the ceiling.

"But—"

Before I could form a sentence, the woman on her left tugged at my hand while the one on her right protested and pushed my shoulders, forcing me to sit beside my grandmother.

"Let her be," the second woman ordered. "Where're you dragging her to?"

"But we can't tell her now. It's too fresh," the other one countered.

"When do you want to tell her then? The moment she steps out of here, someone else will tell her. She's not a little child anymore. We have to tell her now."

They went back and forth a few more times, acting as though I was invisible or even worse, stupid. I already knew something terrible had happened. Amidst the chaos, all I was thinking was that I could bear almost anything as long as it had nothing to do with my grandfather.

"It's your grandfather," the two women said in unison, while my grandmother stared mindlessly with her head stooped to one side.

"He is gone," she added. Her wailing had stopped. She replaced it with sniffling and heaving as she watched me with eyes that revealed the deepest sorrow I had ever seen.

* * *

The news devastated me. The love I had for my grandfather knew no bounds, and my mind never imagined a world without him. Frozen to the spot, I stared in front of me as my grief filled my insides. Coughing to clear a lump in my throat, I fell on my knees and gasped for breath. Ifedi yelled my name and ran to my side, grabbing my hand and dragging me to my room while I tugged my school bag with my free hand. After she shut the door behind us, I sat on my bed and stared at the wall.

"I don't think it's true that Papa's gone," I said after a few minutes had passed. I was sure that if what I'd heard was the truth, I would have had a premonition about it. Since that hadn't happened, I held on to the slight chance that I was having a nightmare.

"Where do you think he is then?"

"I was hoping you'd tell me."

The moment my mouth uttered those words and a steady stream of tears ran down my cheeks, I felt as though my heart was sinking into a deep, dark hole. I remember the feeling of hopelessness like it was yesterday.

Before Ifedi could open her mouth, Okem, who had been living with us for over a year, walked into the room. His eyes were red and puffy, and his teeth chattered while his chest heaved convulsively.

I repeated my question to Ifedi and waited for her to respond, praying she chooses her words with care. Being on the edge, I knew the slightest thing could throw my already fragile being overboard. I still hoped what I'd seen out there in my grandmother's parlor was a figment of my imagination.

Ifedi had taken too long to respond. My head, still reeling to the point I became unaware of my immediate surroundings, I threw my back on the bed.

The sorrow had engulfed me and pushed me beyond the boundaries of my being. It was right there and then that I entered Luenah for the first time.

* * *

I'd found myself walking down a narrow path, bordered by trees on both sides that formed a canopy over my head. Orange streaks filtering through the gaps in the trees formed abstract patterns on the ground, which created an optical illusion. I'd felt a gentle breeze blow across my face, tickling my nostrils and forcing a sneeze. As I began to inhale and appreciate the serenity the surroundings offered my aching heart, I saw an orangutan jumping from branch to branch. I followed it with my eyes and lost track of my steps for a moment. Not realizing I had reached the tail end of the path, I continued walking and entered a seemingly different world, landing on a trail near a seashore. My grandfather was right there, waiting to take my hand. Shocked to see him after just hearing he had died, I trembled and remained fixed to the spot.

"Ona, it's me," he said, looking down to smile at me.

"Papa," I cried, hugging him as tears rolled down my cheeks.

We held hands and walked in silence for a few minutes before we came upon the shimmering sea.

"Where is this, Papa?" I had asked, finally

garnering the courage to speak. "Where are we? Why did you leave? Answer me, Papa," I demanded, tugging gently on his robe.

"Good things come to those who wait," he had responded in a monotone. "You must be patient."

Surprisingly, I obeyed.

We got to a narrow street, and I realized this world did not belong to only me and my grandfather. There were all kinds of people, in all shades, colors, and sizes. There were people everywhere: on the streets; in the market; in the field; and even in the sky, hovering in large aircrafts. A variety of marine mammals leaped in and out of the ocean. Business and trading and playing and partying and anything you could imagine went on in Luenah. Merchants exchanged goods and traded both physical and intangible items, speaking in a language that to my amazement I could speak fluently too.

I stood and pondered this mystical world I had found myself in.

"You're in Luenah," my grandfather said.

"Luenah?"

It had felt natural when I arrived at this place. It was a place of infinite possibilities. A place I could never have realized had I remained standing on the other side—in the dream. I had been close to accessing this portal in the past, but something had always held me back. I had been afraid of what I would find if I went all the way in. This time, though

I was summoned by an indescribable force, I had entered with ease. Something about the grief from losing my grandfather gave me the courage I needed to enter the narrow passage to Luenah. The second I stepped in, I knew I had made the right decision. I immediately felt at peace; all fear was gone.

* * *

After we'd walked for miles, it seemed like there was zero conflict in Luenah. It appeared pure. Bordering towns spoke the same language and in the same dialect. No communication was lost in translation. The boundaries were not defined, but everyone seemed to know what those boundaries were and respected them, unlike Ide and Ntebe, with their unending clashes and disagreements with each other and the neighboring towns. My real world hadn't always been like that, though. Due to colonization, the demarcation of boundaries for Ide, a beautiful coastal town bustling with trade and amusement, and its neighboring Ntebe had occurred haphazardly, without considering the wishes of the people, and the standing issues and agreements. In contrast, Luenah was perfect, exhilarating, and full of peace. Everyone worked in harmony.

No one seemed to have noticed my grandfather and me. People went about their business as though they didn't know we existed. My grandfather looked different, not like the Papa I used to know. He looked exactly like he did many years ago, in the pictures I saw in my grandmother's old album. "Pictures from before the war," my grandmother had called them. They were taken when my grandfather was fair and limber. As he grew older, his skin had darkened from aging and exposure to the sun, and wrinkles formed around his eyes from years of deep smiles.

We arrived at a corner store near a pristine beach. A large carriage with wheels with a mind of its own stopped in front of us and its antique-style door opened by itself. I glimpsed a magical space, as magical as the world we were about to leave behind. I hesitated for a second and then recalled how my hesitance had deprived me of Luenah for years, so I let go of my doubts and lugged myself inside.

The carriage was larger than it had seemed from the outside. It had luminescent glass for windows and crystals for ceilings. The walls were made of a glossy material that glistened and provided a view of the beauty of the trees, the sky, and the buildings on the path we traveled. It was a moving theatre that displayed all the pleasure and happiness in Luenah, all at once. I realized that my fears had only prevented me from opening up to a place of joy and complete peace.

"C-can I?" I asked, my hands a few inches from the wall. I wanted to feel everything; to find out how real they were.

"Of course you can."

I walked around, touching different parts as the vehicle moved. The speed in the carriage increased, very much like a roller coaster. We crested the hill and remained suspended for a few moments, only to descend and repeat the process all over again. I was thrilled beyond imagination as I explored all the corners while trying hard not to fall. In the distance, I spotted a huge castle, capped by four towers, blending into the sky behind it to produce an illusion of even greater height.

"That is the shrine," my grandfather said, as though he'd read my mind.

"I've never seen anything this huge," I replied. "It's magnificent."

"It's the seat of office in Luenah. Everything you can imagine happens there. Laws are made and executed, gory confrontations are settled, and innumerable wars have been won with little interference to the inhabitants."

I stared at him in awe, pondering which of the many thoughts moving around in my head was the most appropriate to ask at that moment.

"Who lives there?"

"The supreme ruler and members of his cabinet. And visitors, lots of people streaming in and out of Luenah every day."

"Can we go there?"

"That's where we're headed?"

I smiled, my excitement rising as we hit each

peak.

We rode the entire day, past many streams, rivers, and mountains. I noticed that for however long we rode, darkness never came. I wanted to ask my grandfather why but decided to sit quietly and observe. *Maybe there's no nighttime in Luenah.* Towards the end of the day, we came upon the enigmatic shrine. My grandfather and I dismounted, and he thanked our driver in the language we'd been speaking the whole day.

"What language is that, Papa?"

"The language of Luenah."

"How come I understand it even though I'm just hearing it for the first time?"

He laughed a little and took my hand. "Because you're a member. You're an *Eri*. Members are born knowing the language in their hearts," he'd said, pointing gently at the left side of my chest.

"How did I—I mean when did I become an *Eri*?" I asked wide-eyed.

"It started several millennia ago when Luenah was restricted to its original inhabitants—a handful of people living in utmost serenity and joy, never growing old or dying from diseases. Everything changed when a wily princess, *Ani*, found her way in through a portal in an ant hole. When she arrived in Luenah, panting from exertion, our ruler had taken pity and accepted her into our fold. With time, she proved to be loyal and imaginative, wildly so, that she found immense favor in his eyes, but she wanted more."

"What did she want?" I urged.

"For her people on earth to inhabit Luenah. At the time, the earth was plagued with famine and diseases, and she felt Luenah would provide the respite they needed. As noble as the idea was, it wasn't feasible."

"Why not? There's enough space here for everyone," I claimed, looking around at the beauty and riches in Luenah.

"There's enough space," he agreed. "But there is no room in Luenah for conflict and turmoil. Look at Ide and Ntebe. See what has become of them."

I nodded once, and he continued.

"A few years passed, and Ani presented her plea again. She threatened to expose the ant hole so her people could enter if our ruler failed to grant even a few 'chosen ones' access to live here."

"Did they fall for it?" I asked, my heart beating in anticipation.

"The negotiation was tough, but they later struck a deal. Ani was permitted to select a handful of good earthly humans to visit Luenah. These humans, called *Eris*, were bestowed gifts to be passed on to chosen ones in their future generations, and they were assigned missions to help the earth regain its balance."

"So, *Eris* are born?"

"Yes. Now, instead of an ant hole, each *Eri* is provided access to Luenah through their *chi*, personal spirit. The *Eri's chi* is far more sensitive than normal. This trait allows it to take a human form to be transported to Luenah to live and interact using the same persona as the earthly being."

I sighed deeply, in awe of everything I'd just heard. "Tell me more…"

"You'll understand everything in due time. For now, all you need to know is that many are called, but only a few of us ever make it into Luenah."

"Why not? Why can't everybody make it?"

"Doubt. It's as simple as that. Few have the courage to go through that narrow path, the same way many people shy away from pursuing their goals. They come close enough to get a glimpse but do not take the leap because of fear and doubt. With courage, you can feel the fear and still forge on. It's the vessel that keeps you going."

"How come I never found the courage on my own to come before now? I am quite the explorer, never afraid to climb trees, race boys, or even swim at the stream."

"We're most courageous at our weakest; when we believe we have faced what we fear the most and have nothing more to lose. The news of my passing weakened you and forced you to move. Courage created an urgent need in you to see what was on the other side."

"I'm not sure I understand, Papa."

"It's rare for one to find courage on their own, but I believe you would have eventually found your way through, with the right motivation. You see, courage and motivation are sister traits. The former is devoid of thought and requires extenuating circumstances to drive action, while the latter requires the will or the desire to succeed and involves thoughtful action."

"I always assumed everyone had the desire to succeed. Don't they?"

"Mostly, yes. But not everyone thinks the right thoughts. Desire is fueled by our thoughts, notwithstanding if the desire was brought on by seeing others succeed or by trying to meet the expectations we have of ourselves."

"Aren't thoughts just that—thoughts?"

"No, they are much more impactful than you can ever know. If you can think of something and your brain can define it with clarity, then you can create it. *Onye kwe, chi ya ekwe.* If one agrees, her spirit will agree also. And once your spirit agrees, the deed is as good as done."

"Just like that?"

"Yes, but it requires great discipline. If not, danger would be lurking in every corner because one or two people had unpleasant thoughts about someone who has done them wrong."

"Oh," I said, shuddering at the thought.

"Your grandmother always said you could achieve anything you put your mind to, right?"

"Yes, she did."

"Well, it's the same concept at work here. The right thoughts create emotions that can impact your physical reality and bring things to life. Manifesting your thoughts in the physical involves the performance of tangible activities that lead to the achievement of goals. The key is to focus most of your energy on those activities rather than on your end goal, to increase the probability of success."

"I hope I can put this into practice."

"Always pray that God honors your efforts and back up that prayer with conducting your affairs with integrity to increase the likelihood of getting those prayers answered."

I stopped for a moment to ponder his words. "This is a lot for me to take in," I said to him.

Although I didn't understand most of the concepts he was trying to teach me at the time, I reckoned I would work towards figuring them out by myself.

"Come, there's something I have to show you," he said, beckoning to me.

For some reason, I couldn't explain, my heart raced, and I held my chest and hoped my heartbeat wasn't as loud to him as it was to me.

* * *

We were standing at the door of the shrine. Towering over us, it was at least three times my grandfather's height. He picked up the large brass knocker, shaped like the head of a lion, and banged it against the door once.

"Take off your shoes," he said, taking my hand while we waited for an answer.

"Why, Papa?"

"Because it's forbidden to get past this point wearing footwear from the outside."

Seconds after I kicked off my shoes, the door flew open, and we took a step forward. Before I got the chance to peep inside, my grandfather let my hand slip away after muttering something indecipherable.

"What?" I asked in frustration.

No answer.

"Papa," I cried out.

No answer. My grandfather had vanished. The numbing pain I felt from his loss filled my heart again.

CHAPTER THREE

I **HAD WOKEN** up to the sound of my
grandmother's voice calling me.

"Ona... Ona... Ona."

My head still reeling to the point that I was
quivering, I slowly opened my eyes. As I massaged
my temples to relieve the tension in my head, the
memory of my visit to Luenah immediately came
back to me. My grandfather had been trying to reveal
something important, I'd believed. I regretted that my
grandmother had brought me back before I found out
what it was. She was clutching the bed frame and
heaving a sigh of relief while I sat upright and
surveyed the room. Ifedi and Okem were standing
right behind her. They both seemed perplexed. Two
of my grandmother's friends, who had been rolling
on the floor, wailing, were standing at the foot of the

bed, their chests heaving wildly.

"Thank God!" the first woman exclaimed. "How would your grandmother have survived another tragedy, *eh*?" she said, raising both hands in the air.

The second woman clapped her hands and twisted her lips.

"God forbid!" she said. "Don't scare your grandmother like that again, *inugo*? Have you heard?"

I stared angrily at them, as they looked at me with trepidation. *Why did they have to be so dramatic? I thought to myself.*

"Open your mouth and speak," the second woman yelled.

"I wasn't trying to scare anybody," I muttered. "I was just sleeping."

"Sleeping?" my grandmother asked with a questioning glance. "Ifedi said you collapsed on your bed, and she couldn't wake you."

I looked at Ifedi, and she nodded slowly.

"I was too tired," I protested. "I must have fallen into a deep sleep."

"If that is all, no problem," my grandmother said. "I was just about to send for the doctor. There's no need for that now. Ifedi, find this girl something to eat and make sure she drinks plenty of water. She must be dehydrated."

I sighed as I watched her walk out of the room

with the two women, their large buttocks swaying from left to right as they exited.

I was happy my grandmother had bought my excuse—I didn't want to share my experience in Luenah with anybody. Not yet, at least. It was too fresh. Too sweet. And no one would have believed me, anyway. They probably would've labeled me crazy and taken me to the hospital for an evaluation.

"You were just there, like this," Ifedi said, placing her hands over her head to mimic a trance-like state.

"Stop," I pleaded. Her eyes had remained closed for what seemed like an eternity. I couldn't bear to watch her theatrics. "How long was it? How long was I gone?"

"It happened suddenly, and it lasted five whole minutes. I called your grandmother after Okem and I tried to wake you, and you wouldn't budge."

Five minutes seemed like such a short time considering it felt like I'd been in Luenah for a whole day. Although my grandmother had seen me go in and out of reverie and understood my intuitive nature, five minutes was much longer than anything she'd ever witnessed. She had seemed like the calmest person in the room, but I knew the incident had frightened her, considering she also had to grapple with my grandfather's passing. If I hadn't returned when I did, she might have lost control.

"You scared all of us," Ifedi said, disrupting my

thoughts.

"I'm sorry for the trouble I caused."

"It's not your fault. You heard what your grandmother said. Come with me and get some food."

We passed a multitude of people to get to the kitchen where Ifedi gave me a small mango to eat while she prepared a meal for me. I reminisced about my experience and was tempted to tell her about it but changed my mind each time the idea cropped into my head. My adventure in Luenah was the most spectacular thing that had ever happened to me up until that moment. I was determined to keep it all to myself until it felt safe to reveal to anyone—until the risk of being dragged to the insane asylum no longer existed.

* * *

Papa's burial was in June. The weather that day had been pleasant. It had rained a little in the morning, but by noon the skies had cleared. The occasion was like nothing I'd ever seen. Hordes of people zoomed into my grandfather's palatial compound and filled all the rooms and balconies. Others settled down in plastic chairs under the canopies that covered the grounds. Some sought shade under the mango trees, and the market square also became an extension of the house as the massive compound could not possibly accommodate all the people in attendance.

Death was nothing new to me as living with my grandparents gave me the experience of witnessing village elders passing away. My grandfather was always in attendance to support families who had lost loved ones, and I sometimes accompanied him. Unlike the others, his death was more than a passing experience. This was no ordinary man. This was my Papa—a six-foot-six gentle giant, the head of our family. Since my grandfather was a chief, layers of rites were performed in keeping with the tradition of Ntebe. All the other chiefs in the town, twenty in total, lined up in their full chiefly regalia to pay homage to their fallen comrade. For a full twenty minutes, they danced and made ritualistic sounds around the casket that bore the body of my grandfather. I remember being in complete awe of their attires and flamboyant displays.

They placed the casket in the ground at midday. I stood next to my grandmother and my parents at the graveside. My parents had been in Ntebe since the day before. For the first time that day, I saw a physical reaction from my grandmother. Wailing from deep within her lungs, she threatened to throw herself into the six-foot grave if my grandfather didn't return to her. As the gravediggers worked desperately to cover the hole with a mound of red dirt, a group of men tried to prevent her from jumping in.

"Stop her!" I heard several people screaming.

Since I had always known her to be dramatic, I doubted she was going to carry out her threat. And I was right. As gunshots to commemorate the occasion tore through the air, my grandmother abandoned her display and ran for cover.

After the ceremony outside was concluded, my grandmother, Okem, and I headed upstairs to the parlor. The merriment continued outside and gradually progressed inside. People came and never left, crowding the entire compound. Drinks, food, and more food created the atmosphere of a festival. Everyone settled down to eat their plates of *jollof* rice and goat meat and consume bottles of beer and soft drinks. The VIPs were led inside to partake of a feast, one worthy of 'big men'. They were provided a spread with a selection of up to twelve different dishes that included *isi-ewu*, plantain porridge, rice with stew, *ukwa*, a variety of meat and fish, pounded yam, and various types of soup. They also had an assortment of drinks at their disposal and were served by uniformed waiters assigned to attend especially to them.

As I walked around observing the festivities, I noticed that everyone seemed to have the same goal: *fun*. I bent my head in embarrassment as I walked past groups of people fighting for how to share some money or farm animal—chicken, goat, or cow. I remember thinking they were ridiculous for having fun at my grandfather's expense.

My grandmother had returned to her position on the sofa, and women wearing *aso-ebi*, uniformed attires, surrounded her. They barely spoke. Unlike the visitors outside, making merriment and eating, tradition prohibited her from touching a drop of food—not while his body was warm in the ground—a show of respect for her dead husband. People came by, each whispering a few words at a time and then placing an envelope I assumed contained money onto the plate in front of her. She neither smiled nor nodded throughout.

"When will all these people leave?" I asked Ifedi as evening came, and it became rowdier.

"Not for another three days."

"Three days!" I exclaimed.

* * *

As I looked at the sea of faces in our home—people here to support my family as my grandfather once supported theirs—I heard their voices of sympathy, wonderment, laughter, and hope and wondered how they really viewed him. What memories did they conjure when they thought of him? My heart was heavy as I pondered this question before my eyes finally rested on Okem.

"Ona," Okem called, cutting through my reverie and taking my hand.

We walked into my grandfather's parlor, where several people were seated, and found a corner to ourselves.

"Are you missing your grandfather," he asked, wiping a tear from the corner of my eye.

I nodded furiously. No one had cared to ask me that important question, not even my parents, who were fully engrossed in the activities themselves. I had spoken to them over the phone three times since my grandfather passed and saw them for the first time in seven months when they arrived for the funeral.

"I miss my Papa," I said, sobbing.

"Don't cry," Okem said. "You're not alone. The three of us will make a good team; me, you, and your grandmother."

I turned slightly to glance at him. The look I saw in his eyes was so warm, so sincere, and so genuine. I knew I could trust him.

"And grandfather," I added.

"Yes. Your grandfather, too. He can be part of our team."

"Do you really believe that?" I'd asked, looking at him incredulously, certain he had said that just to appease me.

"The chief was not my father, but I loved and admired him for taking me into your family. He took care of me as his own. Of course I want him to be part of our team. I only avoided mentioning him because he's gone, and we'll never see him again."

"I have seen him," I blurted out.

"Where?" he'd asked, staring at me with his mouth agape.

I sighed and hesitated for a moment, unsure whether to throw all caution to the wind and trust him completely.

"In Luenah," I said.

I was already convinced that Okem loved my grandfather almost as much as I did. Since I'd been itching for an opportunity to tell someone that I'd seen him in Luenah, I took the bait.

"Where is Luenah?"

He spoke loudly.

"Shh!"

I told Okem about my experience in Luenah—everything that had happened from the moment I got there to when I left. I described the shrine, the carriage, the towns, the people, as well as the many traditions I witnessed there. I even shared with him the valuable lessons I'd learned from my grandfather. By the time I finished, he was grabbing my arm, a bit too tightly, with astonishment written all over his face.

"Ouch!"

"I'm sorry," he said, releasing my arm.

"Promise to never breathe a word about this to another," I said, looking deep into his eyes.

"I promise," he responded, crossing his fingers.

* * *

Okem, my grandmother, Ifedi, and I lived in peace from then on. The bond Okem and I developed at my grandfather's funeral grew stronger. Love for my grandfather and the secret we now shared connected us more than I could ever have imagined. He accompanied me everywhere—church, sports games, and even birthday parties, and he protected me with every ounce of his being. Once, we were at a birthday party where the host's dog chased me down the gate. Okem ran after the dog to get it to stop. After pushing me to the ground, the dog turned away from me and jumped on him, barking and scratching his face while he fought hopelessly to defend himself. I remember screaming for someone to save Okem. It was barely one year after my grandfather died, and the pain of his loss was still too fresh. I couldn't bear to lose another person I cared about. Nothing else mattered at that moment, not my leg, which was bleeding from scraping on the concrete floor, nor my hair, which was now in shambles, and not even the fact that other kids were staring at us with terrified looks on their faces. I screamed at the top of my lungs, and within seconds, two men and two women ran towards us. The men subdued the dog and set Okem free. One of the women pulled me off the ground as the other smoothed my clothes and wiped the tears running down my face. Amidst all that chaos, Okem lifted me with both hands and walked in the direction of the house. Everyone stared at us in amazement. Okem had grown from the scrawny child that came to live with us a few years back to a strong teenager. I couldn't believe it was the same person who had irritated me so much the first time I met him that sacrificed his own life to save me.

* * *

Before long, Okem became my greatest friend, confidant, and teacher. My grandmother sent Okem to the community secondary school in Ntebe, and I moved away from home to attend the private co-ed in Ajidi, the big city. Okem's school wasn't highly ranked, but it was relatively good. It had produced some high caliber individuals that went on to become successful leaders in the community. In contrast, my school was one of the highest-ranked schools in Ajidi. It was reserved for the brightest and the most privileged pupils—the children of the rich, and top government officials.

Despite the differences in our upbringing, Okem and I treated each other as equals. I wished I could see him every day I was in school. Unfortunately, that luxury was left for the holidays and once a term when he came along with my grandmother on visiting days. On those special occasions, Okem dressed in his Sunday best and wore his hair in a different hairstyle each time to impress me—whatever was in style that season. The haircuts always had a name— "pompadour" or "high top fade," or "mohawk." It was always something funny. I could sense his excitement whenever he showed them off. Those occasions were the most memorable of my stay in boarding school.

Okem was a day-student, so he was always at home whenever I came back for the holidays. We played and explored the city and visited friends. Sometimes, we stayed indoors and watched movies all day long. When the holidays were over, and we needed to part ways, we found it difficult to let go of each other. I would cry and Okem would look for a way to soothe me and remind me that come visiting day, he would be there in his Sunday best and a brand new haircut. That calmed me down immediately.

CHAPTER FOUR

MY TRANCE THE day my grandfather died marked the beginning of my adventures in Luenah. I went in and out a few more times and never could explain what got me there. All I knew was that I often drifted to Luenah when I felt down, either from missing my grandfather or being confronted with a problem I couldn't solve. To an observer, it seemed like I was in deep slumber, although it never felt that way to me. I could always differentiate my sleeping state from the other dimension. Luenah was worlds apart from mine. With a population of about a hundred thousand, including animals and cryptic beings, this place fascinated me as much as it fulfilled me. In Luenah, I allowed myself to explore. I addressed my doubts and fears and interacted with the people I met in this mystical world. Soon, I started to refer to it as my place of utmost serenity. A place I felt most at peace. But never again was I able to see my grandfather until the day I turned eighteen.

* * *

I was sitting in my room staring into space, my thoughts shifting in every direction when I suddenly slipped into a dream. I followed the narrow path and eventually landed in Luenah. Like the gleaming sea, the golden hue cast by the sunset over the rolling hills took my breath away. I followed the path to the road and walked for several miles until I arrived at a grassy field that stretched out, unbroken, to the skyline. I cleared a spot and lay on my back. Facing the sky, I pondered the beauty of the surroundings as the sweet scent of flowers wafted through my nostrils. Sighting the carriage a few feet away, I stumbled towards it, my legs still numb from all the walking. I took a seat by the window after greeting the driver. We rode for hours, past many towns and rivers, but for some reason I couldn't comprehend, the roads and the markets were deserted. The shops, including the little antique shop I frequently visited with a friendly elderly couple, had a closed sign on their doors. The pace of my breathing increased when in the distance, I saw the majestic peaks of the shrine—a place I was yet to enter despite my frequent visits—and reckoned we were heading in that direction. My excitement grew as I imagined who I was going to meet, what I was going to see, and all I was going to do. I had missed my chance to go past the doors the day my grandfather died; my grandmother's hysterics had shaken me back to reality.

* * *

From the outside, the shrine was colossal. I wasn't sure I would be allowed inside without my grandfather by my side. But as soon as I kicked off my shoes and banged on the brass knocker, the door flew open, and I entered with ease. I carefully navigated the roomy hallways that led to another ancient-style door that opened the moment I stopped in front of it. It was as if I was being summoned by a force greater than me. I glided past a bridge crafted with copper and silver, with the handles made of gold. The walls were made from stained glass. The ceilings bore carvings of beasts, some from the real world, others I had never seen or heard of before. They seemed to come alive as the carvings projected from the top. Strange creatures moved around in pairs. A growl startled me, causing my heart to almost fall into my mouth as I turned to watch a mysterious creature, the size of two bulls walk stealthily past me. Its body was like that of a man but his head was shaped like an eagle's. Following him was a feline creature with two human heads. I could hear the faint soothing sound of a river running between the rooms. Without knowing the source, I could see it culminated in a waterfall that was clearly within view of the throne room. I observed the people streaming out from different corners. There were many rooms, so many, I couldn't count. On a gilded throne sat a man—his age, hard to decipher, his long, tight curls, flowing down to his chest. A crown of stones sat on his head. His blue robe was cinched at the waist with a gold belt. In his hand was a carved cane, while his shoulders hunched as he waited in anticipation. Flanked on either side of him were lesser dressed men. Some sat at his feet with a look of amazement registered on their faces. The manner with which they gazed and bowed to him, I could tell he was a leader of sorts, and they were his subjects. A king most likely, judging from how everyone did his bidding. As men and women were called, they walked humbly towards him and made their requests. I remained in awe, unsure of why I was there, until I saw my grandfather heading from the direction of the rooms, a huge smile plastered on his face as he approached me.

"Papa—" I had begun to say when the King announced, "Today is your day," in the same stentorian voice I'd heard him speak with all evening.

I looked around at the crowd that had increasingly gathered and wondered how I was expected to respond. I was in awe of the magnificent King and afraid the wrong answer would tick him off.

I waited for my grandfather to give me a cue, but he maintained his stance and avoided looking in my direction.

"Bring that thing," the King continued after some time had elapsed.

What thing? I looked around excitedly, trying to figure out what he could have been talking about. The throne room was full by this time, and everyone watched with excited looks on their faces. Their silence amazed me. Not a single person was breathing or shuffling their feet. They were in as much awe of the King's presence as I was. Or perhaps it was something else. I wasn't sure. I redirected my gaze to my grandfather and noticed he was holding a mysterious looking vintage box, the size of a large encyclopedia, in his hand.

"Could this be my birthday gift?" I muttered under my breath.

"Don't speak unless you've been spoken to," my

grandfather chided quietly before handing me the box. "Open it."

It was then I realized I had been summoned to the King's presence to celebrate my birthday. Later, I learned my birthday had been pronounced a holiday in Luenah, which explained why everywhere was deserted on my way to the shrine.

"Open it," my grandfather repeated.

"Now? In front of everybody?"

"Yes! You should open it now."

I heeded his instruction and opened the box.

"It's empty," I said, looking at him and wondering if he had planned to play a trick on me. I was counting on his eyes to start dancing with amusement, my cue it'd been a joke. Nothing. I giggled nervously. Still, nothing.

He maintained a serious look on his face.

"What do you see inside?" he asked.

I looked from the box and then to my grandfather and then to the box again. The only thing inside was packing tissue and a little sprinkle of crystals. I shifted my gaze from him to the King and then to the subjects in the throne room. Everyone seemed composed and unmoved by the surprised look on my face.

"You have now come of age to go after your purpose," my grandfather said. "This box is your gift. It will receive what you have to give in exchange."

"If it's my gift, why do I need to give

something?"

"Things work a little differently in Luenah. Since you've been chosen to be a member, you have to give something in return. To embark on your mission—"

"Go on. Enlighten her," the King's voice boomed, shaking the ground underneath me.

My grandfather nodded once.

"Remember what I told you about Ani?" he said.

"I do. I remember it clearly. That was when I found out I was an *Eri*. I remember that first visit to Luenah as though it was yesterday."

"Well, to honor Ani's request to allow earthly humans into Luenah, she was mandated to exchange something valuable."

"What could she have given in exchange?"

"She was forced to give up access to Luenah, a place she loved beyond imagination. She spent the rest of her days interceding for her people and bringing balance back to earth. Just like Ani, every *Eri* must surrender something important as they embark on their mission to give something back to humanity."

My eyes darted to the box in my hand as I pondered the meaning behind his assertions and what I was expected to give in exchange.

"What about me? What am I expected to give?" I finally asked after I found the courage to speak.

"It is for you to discover. You'll figure it out on

the path to discovering your purpose."

"My purpose?"

"Yes. Once you discover it, you'll be on your way to accomplishing your assignment in Luenah. Start by asking yourself what you care about the most. Do you know what that is?"

He was looking down at me as he waited for an answer.

I took a moment to consider what the best response could be in these pristine surroundings. Besides being with my family, there were only two things I craved more than anything else in this world.

"Love and happiness," I said, certain it was best to be completely honest.

To my surprise, everyone in the throne room, except for my grandfather, laughed.

"That's what I care about the most in this world," I whined, embarrassed, and disappointed that they found my desires amusing.

"In that case," my grandfather continued amidst the chatter, "think carefully before you surrender yourself or anything as it may affect the joy of your pursuit. And keep in mind what I told you the first time we met in Luenah—that it doesn't matter when you get to your destination. What matters is that you enjoy the journey. When you surrender the goal, you'll enjoy the journey more"

I shook my head repeatedly to make it obvious I still needed clarification.

"You'll understand in due time," he said with a chuckle. "I'll leave something with you, though. Try not to focus on finding happiness. Doing so may leave you disappointed in the end. The choices one makes on the quest for happiness may end up causing distress after the goal has been achieved. Rather, focus on finding your passion—a key requirement for living a purposeful life."

"My passion?"

"As your grandfather told you, you'll understand everything in due time," the King said, gesturing to one of his guards to usher me out of his presence.

* * *

I was back to earth before I could utter a word in response. My grandfather's words still rang in my ears after I returned to reality. I couldn't believe all I'd just heard. I considered the fact that I was an *Eri* a blessing, and since it explained the reveries and visions since I was a kid, I felt a greater sense of self than I had ever known in my life. That encounter was the first time I ever wondered if I would fulfill my purpose or if I even knew for sure what my purpose was on earth. I always knew that I wanted to be a big shot lawyer, but from what I learned in this visit, it may or may not have something to do with my purpose. Considering my mission as an *Eri* was tied directly to this purpose, I became extremely agitated.

I didn't want to be responsible for disrupting the balance in Luenah if I failed in accomplishing that mission, whatever it may be. From my understanding, doing so could also disrupt the balance on earth. I stopped short when I remembered the importance of the 'exchange' I was supposed to give, something I would only find out on the path to discovering my purpose. I shook my head to make sense of everything that was going on inside of it. Since my grandfather had mentioned I would understand in due time, I reminded myself to be patient. It was only then that I relaxed and got ready to celebrate turning eighteen.

CHAPTER FIVE

"COME IN," I yelled after a loud knock on my door drew my attention from my thoughts. My meeting with Grandfather still clouding my senses, I pulled the covers over my shoulders and waited patiently to see who it was. I almost froze when Okem gingerly walked in, holding a bouquet he had picked from my grandmother's garden with both hands, a cheerful smile plastered across his face. Looking dark and mysterious, his eyes bored through mine as though to savor the joy he knew his gift was bound to deliver. I had been suppressing feelings for him for a while—a fact I was confronted with during this encounter. The look he gave me, which I returned with equal fervor, was different from any I had ever shared with him, or with anyone else for that matter. It felt nice and safe. As he handed me the bouquet and kissed my cheeks, the butterflies in my stomach fluttered noiselessly as my body slowly warmed up. I was certain my face was red even though the coloring wouldn't have been visible through my brown skin.

"Thank you, Okem," I said, looking up at him.

"You're welcome, my dear. Happy birthday to you! Wishing you many more blissful years."

"Thank you," I whispered, sniffing the flowers. "These are gorgeous."

"Ona," he called, startling me. "You've become truly beautiful," he said. "Your eyes..."

"What about them?" I asked, wrinkling my nose.

"They're the most gorgeous things I've ever seen. And those legs..."

"Okem stop!" I said, giggling.

"No problem. What I'd like you to know is when you're older, and I've made something of myself, really made it, I'll ask you to marry me."

Wide-eyed, I laughed, turning my face away and pulling the covers over my head with my free hand.

Okem removed the covers and smiled at me, his eyes revealing so much tenderness and conviction at the same time. The combination of the two disarmed me.

"You're serious?" I said, almost choking on my words.

"You don't believe me?"

"Don't you have to finish school first?"

"I know…I know," he said in a serious tone and then chuckled softly as he took my hand and gently caressed it with his thumb. "You have to trust that I meant every word of it."

I adjusted myself on the bed and discreetly rolled my eyes. My skin still a bit flushed, I sought to deflect his marriage chatter but words failed me.

"Anyway, what are we doing for your birthday?" Okem continued.

I let go of my bashfulness and looked up at the exceptionally handsome man standing next to me. His arms and square shoulders radiated strength, and he possessed a quiet confidence which made him even more attractive to me. It was the first time I'd ever viewed him this way. As I continued to stare, he took the bouquet from my hand, and with purpose and authority, he walked towards the writing desk and placed it in an empty vase he saw sitting there. With his back turned away from me, I cracked my brain about this mysterious boy—no, man—that came into my life not even up to a decade ago. *How mischievous he must be to talk to me about marriage.* But there was nothing mischievous about the way he said it. And his smile afterwards? That floored me.

My mind flew to the first time Okem came to live with us. He was the strangest little thing I'd ever seen. I recalled how he used to fight the other kids— the bullies—who made fun of his clothes. And how all those insults didn't stop him from wanting to hang around me all the time. With these differences between us—our status, birthright, and so on—the love we had for each other remained intact. With time, I viewed him differently from how other people saw him. He often told me he was a prince, and I remember making a paper crown for him using cereal boxes and watercolor. He wore it gallantly while we played. It was all fun and games for me, but Okem took those games seriously, and he got annoyed when I laughed at his impression of a prince.

Okem and I had remained close until I turned thirteen and my body started filling out. That was the year he turned sixteen. From then on, my grandmother began keeping a watchful eye on us. The day I saw my first period, she invited me to her room and made me sit right beside her on the bed. She'd pulled my earlobe and told me everything she felt I needed to survive from then on. It was mostly things I needed to avoid. No boys, no this, no that. Okem bore the brunt of it. He could no longer play in my room, but I was okay with that. My body had gone through radical changes, ones that I found embarrassing, which made me need more space than ever. And with my hourly mood swings, I became less fun to hang around.

* * *

By the time Okem was completing his final year at

university, I was in my second year studying for a Law degree. Still, we remained fond of each other. His school was an hour's drive away from mine, but he always visited me once a week to hang out. We would go shopping, dining, and to the movies, and at the end of each semester, he drove me home for the holidays. My dependence on Okem increased by the day as I relied on him for everything. Our lives, and sometimes our thoughts, were intertwined. We finished each other's sentences and understood each other's moods with little verbal communication. He was my best friend. Strange how this boy whose presence I once rejected and rebelled against any form of friendship with, had become a major part of my life.

My grandmother noticed our closeness. She saw it as adorable at first, but over the years, as our special bond developed, she realized we were too old for our relationship to be mistaken as platonic any longer.

"How is Okem?" she asked, with her brows furrowed after she saw me lying aimlessly on the sofa during the holidays.

"I miss him so much," I said, sighing and retreating into a dream state.

"You miss him *that* much?"

"Yes! He's my best friend. And all my other friends have traveled for the holidays. Had I known this holiday would be like this, I would have stayed back in Ajidi."

"Why Ajidi?"

"To be near him!"

She was taken aback by my response. From her expression afterwards, I could tell something was bothering her. *Have I been completely oblivious to her concerns?* I believed that I had been too forward with my feelings for Okem, but I couldn't help it. It just came out. Okem had been off at school, taking his finals, and I hadn't seen him in a month—a really long time for us to be apart. I was due back to school in three weeks, and there was no telling when I could see him again as he was extremely busy. I didn't think I could bear it any longer, but the truth was, thinking about Okem wasn't the only reason my holiday was turning into a dream fest. My travails in Luenah were top of mind, too. It didn't help that I couldn't go there on my own—I had to be summoned—a sad situation for me because I always got direction and wisdom whenever I visited. But since I couldn't tell my grandmother about Luenah without sounding crazy, I stuck to the topic of Okem.

"Grandma, don't you miss Okem around the house?" I asked. It was my best attempt to cover up my forwardness.

"I do. But not as much as you. I see you moping around every day, and it worries me."

I chuckled and hid my face in embarrassment.

"That reminds me," my grandmother continued, pretending not to notice the effect her words had on me. "Albert's mother asked about you the other day."

"She did?" I asked, pursing my lips.

"Yes. She did." My grandmother was nodding elatedly. "You and Albert seem to get along really well."

"How can you tell?" I asked, smiling in confusion, and resisting the urge to shake my head.

"It's quite obvious." She was grinning.

"Grandma," I yelled in embarrassment.

"Yes?"

"Stop saying such things. I'm not ready for such talk!"

"What do you mean? What do you want me to say?" she responded, shaking her head and raising both hands to the ceiling, as though seeking answers from a divine source. "Look, Ona, you're old enough to marry, and Okem is not on your level, so you may as well get serious about Albert instead of moping around all day. I can't imagine anyone better for you."

My hands had flown to my chest as she was speaking. Her words never failed to surprise me. It was unclear what she meant by "Okem is not on your level," but one thing was clear to me. My grandmother seemed to be encouraging a relationship with Albert—a man I hardly knew.

* * *

Albert was a crown prince—the heir to the throne of

Ide kingdom. Ide, the same town that throughout history has clashed with my people in Ntebe. The clashes had never prevented associations between the two towns as the indigenes had a lot in common, which also made both areas fertile ground for intermarrying. Albert's father, the *Ideme*—the King of Ide—had ruled Ide for so many years, and rumor had it that he planned to hand over the throne to Albert soon. He wanted to ensure a successful transfer of the staff of office to his son, and the only way he could guarantee that was to complete the transfer in his lifetime. Judging from history, a wide range of unexpected circumstances, including attempts to usurp the throne, could obstruct such a transfer if an incumbent king dies without completing the required steps.

My grandmother saw nothing wrong with a union with someone from Ide. Albert was the most eligible bachelor in Ide and Ntebe put together, and he seemed to adore me. I thought Albert was sweet and kind and, as far as looks were concerned, he was tall, with a nice facial structure, although a little too tapered for my liking. The things he had going most for him were his charisma and his wit. He also carried himself with confidence, as is expected for his position. His good qualities, coupled with the fact that he treated me with utmost kindness and respect, encouraged me to throw my misgivings for Ide out of the window.

CHAPTER SIX

MY FIRST MEETING with Albert had been purely accidental. I ran into him. Yes, literally. I was running out of a shop in Ajidi on a rainy night and began crossing the road when his car came to a screeching halt barely two feet away from me. I stood in the middle of the street, stunned at what almost became the end of me when this dark figure took my hand and led me to a safe spot in the corner. The streetlights were off, and high up in the sky was the crescent left over by the waning moon. He muttered something as he tapped me lightly on the cheek to get me out of my daze. The few people who had seen the near-accident stood by, watching and chattering.

"Give her room to breathe," Albert had pleaded. He had been trying to say something, and the increasingly noisy crowd wouldn't let him hear himself, let alone get across to me.

"Are you okay?"

"Huh?"

"Are you okay?" he repeated slowly.

"I can't hear you."

"Move… move," he pleaded, waving his hand at the crowd.

Some unwillingly dispersed, while a handful meandered still.

"You," Albert said, pointing at me. "I'm not sure what's going on in your mind, but you should have known better than to step out on the street like that." He spoke in a patronizing tone.

At first, I was so bewildered that I could not think of the right words to say to him. I simply peered at him. I did not like this rude stranger at all.

"I should have known *better*?" I whispered when I finally found my voice. "What does that even mean?"

"Hey! I was only trying to help. Calm down!"

"I should calm *down*?" I yelled. What kind of person says that to someone they almost ran over?"

"No one talks to me like that! Does she know who I am?" he asked, shooting a glance at the people standing around.

"Maybe the nearest psychiatrist hospital will have the answer to that question," I said, scoffing at his arrogance.

"What did you say?"

I could have sworn that I saw the veins on his neck popping in the dimly lit street as the people that witnessed the altercation between us chuckled to themselves. Ignoring his rants, I emerged from the horde, but I could feel his eyes watching my back as I jumped into a waiting taxi and headed straight for my hostel.

* * *

The following day, Amah, who was attending the same university in Ajidi, barged into my room as I tried to catch a few minutes of sleep and announced that I had a visitor in the lobby. Standing at five-feet-five-inches tall—the same height as me—Amah's ebony black skin glistened in the midday light as she wiggled her tiny waist in the fitted camisole dress she had on as she spoke.

"Is it the dry cleaner's boy?" I asked, getting out of my bed, happy that the clothes I'd sent for cleaning were finally being delivered.

"Dry cleaner *ke?*" Amah chirped. "Except if the dry cleaner wears a two-thousand-pound designer watch."

"Amah, who is it then? Doesn't this person have a name?"

"He didn't give his name. I heard him asking the caretaker for Ona, and I offered to come and get you. Did I commit a crime?" she asked, chuckling and shaking her head.

"It's probably someone from my grandmother. But she just sent my uncle with some provisions last week. Anyway, I won't put it beyond her to start worrying if I have everything I need so soon after—"

"Ona, believe me," Amah interjected, her tongue still as sharp as ever, "this one is not from your grandmother."

"Then who can it be?"

"Why don't you go down and find out yourself."

"Okay, Amah. I'll be right down."

I took off my robe and threw on some clothes before heading down the stairs leading to the lobby. From a distance, I noticed a tall, svelte stranger in faded blue jeans and a black dress shirt waiting patiently with his car keys dangling in his hand. The dark shadows from the night before had obscured his features, but as I got closer, I recognized Albert. Thinking there had been a mistake, I immediately turned on my heel, but he strode forward and stopped right in front of me, blocking me from moving.

"Hey, Ona," he said.

"Excuse me?" I responded, attempting to slide past him as people walking by stopped to look at us.

"Can you at least hear me out?" he pleaded in a soft tone.

"What could you possibly say to me? Haven't you said enough?" I responded.

"At least let me show you how sorry I am."

"Start by telling me how you figured out my name and where to find me."

He chuckled and glanced behind him.

"You're acting like you're not aware that the shop you were stepping out of yesterday is a popular university hangout. Many people knew who you were."

"And they gave you my info?" I asked, staring at him in amazement.

"They knew I wouldn't bite you," he said with a smirk. "I told them I needed to check on you to make sure you were fine after the incident."

In my confusion the day before, I had mistaken him for an ogre and assumed he must have been fifty or so based on his attitude. Now that I could see him in the light and his attitude was changed, I was certain he couldn't be a day over twenty-six.

"I'm sorry for responding so harshly yesterday, and it's nice of you to come and check on me, but I really should take some responsibility for the incident."

"But I ran into you."

"Yes, but I'm the one who ran into the street mindlessly. I should have looked where I was going."

"Does that mean you accept my apology?" he asked, grinning widely. "Where are your parents? I feel I should meet them and offer an apology."

"Why?" I said, rolling my eyes discreetly. "I live

with my grandparents. My grandmother, actually. In Ntebe. Do you know where that is?"

"Do I know where Ntebe is? We're neighbors. I'm from Ide."

"Ide! Our enemies," I quipped, raising my shoulders in mock disdain.

He laughed and pulled out his phone.

"So, you're my sister? Let me have your number. I'll call you sometime to see how you're doing."

I took his phone from his hand and slowly punched in my number but realized midway I didn't even know his name.

"What's your name?" I asked.

"Albert Ndu."

"Ndu? Are you related to—?"

He was nodding before I could complete my sentence.

"Ndu. The *Ideme*. The King of Ide," he said matter-of-factly.

"Nice to meet you," I hummed, offering my hand to shake and trying my best to seem indifferent. "What are you doing in Ajidi?"

"Trying to earn a living."

"This far away from home?"

"I could say the same about you. Why did you stray so far away?"

"I attended high school in Ajidi. I'm used to the city, so it was a natural choice for University."

He nodded and gave me a warm smile.

"Now that we've discovered we're neighbors, I don't see why we can't be friends."

"It depends," I teased. "Can Ide and Ntebe really be friends?"

"What do you mean?" he asked, creasing his forehead.

I burst out laughing and gestured for him to follow me on a short stroll as I explained the joke.

"So how can I see you again?" he'd asked when we stopped in front of my hostel.

"I don't know," I said, a bit flustered by his request. "Classes will be over in two weeks. I'll be going home right after my exams."

"Alright, we'll make plans then."

* * *

Albert called me every day after that first meeting. At first, it was to check how I was doing. Later, after he knew I was fine, he called to say hi. At least, that's how he put it. I started to look forward to his calls. After I came home for the holidays, he was there to see me the following day, bearing gifts. And he came every single day of the break. My grandmother became fond of him and fell for his great manners and easy charm. She had expected him to be arrogant because of his status, but he appeared sweet and gentle. Although she wasn't one to be moved by influence and success, she thought he would make the perfect husband for me. I could tell she was imagining our potential future together every time she saw me with Albert. The look in her eyes gave her away. But who could blame her? I had slowly developed a sweet spot for Albert, too.

With Okem still at school prepping for his finals, Albert kept me company and helped me forget how much I missed Okem. The second Sunday I was home, he invited me to his church and later to lunch at the palace.

Right in the center of Ide, the palace serves as the official residence and administrative headquarters of the King. Behind the massive wrought iron gate, there were palm trees of the Ceroxylon Quindiuense variety lining the entire circumference of the fence, and impeccable gardens and orchards. I counted five duplexes, each with a unique style ranging from medieval to modern, with entrances lined with stone sculptures that seemed to come to life if stared at for too long. Four bungalow-style homes located at the North end of the duplexes served as servants' quarters.

Inside one of the duplexes, Albert introduced me to his Aunt, Ekema—the King's younger sister. Ekema doted on Albert, but she also took interest in me, asking me about school, my family, and my plans for the future. After lunch, Albert and I played games and walked hand in hand in the garden, talking as though we'd known each other for ages. I couldn't imagine the afternoon could get any more interesting, but I was wrong.

We had just returned from our walk and were relaxing with his aunt and his mother in the living room when the housekeeper announced that I had a guest. I was stunned. The only people that knew I was there were my grandmother and Ifedi, who over the years had ceased being my nanny and assumed several roles, including companion and housekeeper. I prayed there was no emergency since it was unlike either one of them to come looking for me at random.

"Ask the guest to come in," Albert's mother said.

I was stunned when Okem walked in.

"Okem," I shouted, tossing my manners out of the window for a second but resisting the urge to get up and hug him. "I thought you'd be at school. I didn't know you'd come back so soon. How did you know I was here? How did you get here?"

"Your grandmother told me you were here, so I drove from Ntebe to come and see you," he muttered before turning to bow in the direction of Albert's mother and aunt. "Good afternoon."

"Good afternoon," Albert's mother responded. "How are you, my dear? Have a seat."

Okem smiled wryly and shook his head. "No *Ma*, thank you."

"Are you sure?"

"I'm sure, *Ma*," he responded. "I have to go

right away. I just returned from school and wanted to let Ona know I was back since we haven't seen each other in over a month—"

"So you drove all the way from Ntebe just to do that?" Ekema interjected, continually rolling her eyes with disdain toward him.

"I understand you're in a hurry but have a soft drink at least," Albert's mother pleaded before Okem could respond to Ekema.

"No *Ma*, thank you so much. I really appreciate your offer."

"That's alright, my son."

"I'll see him out?" I said, standing from my seat and walking towards the door. I felt the need to stick up for him after the way Ekema had treated him.

"It's so nice to see you Okem," I said as soon as we stepped outside the room. "Once lunch is over, I'll head straight home so we can catch up. And, I'm sorry about Albert's aunt."

He nodded.

"Is everything okay?" I asked. "How are you? How were your exams?"

"Are you sure you care to know?" he scoffed.

"Why not?" I said, stunned by his cold-shoulder. "We've all been anxiously waiting for you to come home."

"Really?"

"Yes! Really."

"Okay. I'll see you later then," he answered

brusquely and walked away.

I took a moment to recover from his snobbery before I returned to the living room, only for Albert to avert his gaze the moment I walked in. His creased forehead revealed his obvious annoyance.

"That was Okem, ma'am," I said, directing my comment to Albert's mother.

"I heard you call his name when he came in. Your grandmother has told us so much about him, how he's been living with you since he was a kid. I didn't realize he was such a grown man. And a handsome one at that. What does he do for a living?"

"He just finished his final year at the university. He studied Finance."

"That's amazing!"

From behind, I could hear Albert scoff.

* * *

Albert was quiet for the rest of the afternoon. He only spoke to me after I bade his family farewell.

"I'll drive you home," he said.

"Thank you," I responded, walking behind him.

"Why do you have to be so close to your help?" he asked after we stepped outside. "I don't understand why he couldn't wait for you to get home. He had to run here and spoil a perfectly nice afternoon."

"Okem is not the help. He's one of my best friends."

"One of your best friends?" he said, casting me a scornful look. "Do you see how he looks at you? That boy loves you, and I'm not sure what gave him the guts to come over here. You shouldn't play among people of all social classes. It's demeaning."

"My grandfather raised him. Technically, we're the same."

"I think you know what I'm referring to, so let's not drag the issue."

I kept silent after realizing the reason for Albert's sudden change of mood. The green-eyed monster had reared its ugly head after Okem showed up. He was angry that I'd spoken to Okem or given him any form of attention at all. We didn't speak for the rest of the ride until we arrived at my grandmother's house.

"Can I pick you up tomorrow? I'd like to take you to the cinema?" he said, as he turned the ignition off.

"I'm not sure. Can I check my schedule and get back to you. I don't think, I-I..."

I hadn't seen Okem in a long time, and I thought I'd be spending the next few days catching up with him, but I dared not tell Albert after what I'd just experienced.

"Because Okem is back?" he asked in a sarcastic tone.

"No!" I responded calmly, turning to look at him.

"Then why?" he demanded.

"I believe we can go to the movies." I conceded, too tired to argue.

"Why did you hesitate at first? We've been having a great time together."

"I wasn't sure if my grandmother had anything planned for tomorrow."

I lied to save face.

"I'll pick you up tomorrow then."

"Okay. Have a good evening," I said, leaving the car defeated

* * *

After Albert left, I leaned on the front door for a moment to ponder his reaction when he saw Okem. If I didn't know any better, I would have said they had known each other before, but I knew that not to be true. Tired of my wandering thoughts, I ran to my room to change before I headed out to look for Okem.

"Okem just left in a huff," Ifedi said when she saw me heading toward his room.

"What do you mean he left in a huff? What happened?"

"I don't know! Are you asking me?" she asked wide-eyed. "Okem left to see you at Albert's right after he returned, but before I knew it, he was back. Didn't you see him?"

"He was there briefly."

"What happened at Albert's? What did you do

to make him so mad?" She was gazing in anticipation.

"I have no clue. I was stunned that he would drive an hour to see me and then leave right away. With the traffic between Ntebe and Ide, that must have been an additional thirty minutes, but I guess—"

"You guess what?" she blurted.

"Never mind," I said. "Did he say where he was going? When he's returning?"

"No, and no. Your grandmother should never have told him you were there. I found out after he'd left, and I had no clue he would come looking for you. Such a—"

"Don't bother," I said, stopping her mid-sentence. I was sure she was about to rain insults on my Okem. What I wasn't sure about was why she was so irritated. If anyone should be upset, it was I, and I wasn't even nearly as perturbed as she was.

"What happened in Ide?"

"He came in briefly but refused to stay. Said something about just having returned and then left. It was an interesting afternoon. I'm tired. I hate dealing with adult tantrums."

"Be very careful, my dear," Ifedi said, shaking her head slightly.

"Why?" I scoffed. "Why is everyone acting so weird?"

"Why are you the only person who doesn't see what's going on? Don't you see how Okem looks at you?"

"Hmm! The same way you, Grandma, or even Albert, look at me. Am I missing something?"

She appeared stunned for a moment.

"Apparently."

"I still don't know what you're talking about, Ifedi. I'll just have to wait for him to come back to resolve this issue."

Okem didn't come back that day. The following day, after I returned from the movies with Albert, he was home, acting as though nothing had happened. He apologized for disappearing, and we spent the next few days catching up like old times and discussing our plans for the future.

* * *

The last week I was home, Okem found another reason to be furious with me. After I came back from watching a soccer game with Albert, he refused to speak to me or even look in my direction. The following day, he apologized, and everything was fine again. As all these things were occurring that holiday—Albert, Okem, Okem's moods, and my grandmother trying to marry me off to the highest bidder—I frequently thought about Luenah, but my chaotic life never gave me any chance to settle down, let alone get teleported there. My last encounter at the shrine never left me, though. Everything my grandfather told me kept coming back to me. My instinct told me that not only were our destinies

connected, but our mission in Luenah could be one
and the same. I couldn't say how, though.

CHAPTER SEVEN

WITHIN MONTHS, THE border clashes between Ntebe and Ide resurfaced. Up to ten riots occurred between the Ntebe-Ide boundary points within a space of one week. The report in Ajidi was quite vivid in its description of what had transpired in the final encounter; rioters tying white cloths around their heads brandished machetes and other dangerous weapons and chanted war calls as they marched through the streets. Without warning, a truckload of youths from the opposing faction jumped out of a moving truck. As both factions attacked each other with their weapons, passersby ran helter-skelter, and the market nearby erupted in fire. Screams of terror filled the air as people dragged their children out of the way. Traders jumped on bikes and moving cars to escape injury. A few stayed back to salvage their wares since it was obvious the market would burn to the ground before the fire service would arrive at the scene. Mobile policemen and riot police arrived as the youths were still wielding their weapons and shouting obscenities at one another. No one had been reported dead yet, but an ambulance carted a number of people to the hospital. Several more were being treated at the scene. The market was still on fire, and the few traders who tried to douse it with buckets of water had long since given up and run for their lives. A gas station nearby had burned to the ground. Fire service had arrived on time to prevent the fire from spreading underground where hundreds of gallons of oil were stored. The police fired gunshots and tear gas into the air to disperse the rest of the warring youth. They ran in every direction, abandoning their truck and other belongings. Only the weak, terribly old, and the injured remained on the scene. The air was so dense with the tear gas and smoke from the fires, it was impossible to see. Several shops along the boundary were looted. Many were vandalized.

It was the end of the final semester of my second year. Albert had been kind enough to drive six hours from Ide to Ajidi to pick me up from school and another six the following day to bring me back home. As he came close to the boundary, I was stunned by the carnage. Unable to breathe from the smoke, I urged him to wind up the windows, but the air was so dense that the smoke still found its way inside the car. The destruction had brought me near tears. Albert saw my pain and placed one hand over my shoulder.

"Don't worry. When I finally take over, I'll put a stop to all this. Will you help me achieve that?"

This was my first time hearing Albert mention his future position.

"What sort of help do you expect from me?" I asked, grateful for his concern.

He turned to look at me, sparking a light in me from the sincerity in his eyes.

"I want you by my side when I'm in charge. Do you think you'd be up to the task?"

"I don't know," I said, shaking my head slowly. "And I'm not sure what you're asking."

"Don't worry. It's not even a good time to bring up that topic. Let's just focus on getting you home safely."

We were only thirty minutes from Ntebe. In the silence that ensued, I pondered Albert's statement and smiled as I imagined what he could have meant. Although the horror of the riot still plagued my mind, I felt I had achieved something meaningful from this experience. Besides the fact that it brought me closer to Albert, it reminded me that I could have a purpose after all. I was still smiling when I heard a loud screeching of tires as Albert swerved dangerously to the right.

"Buffoon," he cursed loudly.

It took a second for me to realize what the issue was. An old man with a wheelbarrow truck had crossed the street without looking, and we almost hit him with our car.

"Oh my goodness!" I exclaimed. "Thank God we didn't run over him."

"This is so ridiculous. There is so much unlawfulness in this town. I hope you're ok," he said, sighing deeply and turning the steering to get back on the road.

* * *

We arrived at Ntebe at the perfect time of day. The sky was streaked with orange clouds that created a beautiful hue on the buildings and the trees. The air, though still stuffy from the remnants of the smoke from the riots, held a promise of rain. I couldn't wait for it to finally come and wash away the residue. Ifedi and my grandmother were waiting at the gate. My grandmother had bags under her eyes, and she appeared dreadfully worried. I knew she would have been trying to reach me. The phone lines had been destroyed by the violent youth. She knew Albert was on his way to pick me up, but she still had her heart in her mouth as she waited anxiously for us to return. When she saw the car driving into the compound, she ran towards us and gave me a big hug soon after I stepped out.

"Thank God," she sighed, throwing her hands in

the air while she performed a small dance. She twisted her waist slowly from side to side before a sad look registered on her face. "Did you see what happened at the boundary?"

I nodded, too tired to speak.

Albert answered for me.

"Terrible devastation. They have arrested the culprits."

"Well, I hope they deal with them thoroughly this time. This sort of thing needs to stop happening," my grandmother responded.

"The youths are just pawns used by the greedy landowners to advance their selfish interests. Someone has to clip their wings, and I'll make sure I discuss this with Father," Albert said.

"I would like to see your father take care of that before things get out of control. Things have really deteriorated since my dear husband passed," she added in a deeply emotional tone. "He and the other chiefs had a way of handling our Ntebe youths to prevent them from going haywire. I don't know what our village head is doing to curtail this problem."

"It will require a joint effort between Ide and Ntebe. We'll form a task force to resolve this, and if that doesn't work, we may have to involve the federal government."

My grandmother nodded her head in agreement. "Come inside. I thank God for bringing my children back safely," she said, flinging her hands in the air.

As Albert opened the trunk to bring out my luggage, Okem stepped inside the compound.

"Okem, you're home," I said excitedly, tears welling up in my eyes.

He greeted Albert cordially with no trace of jealousy or resentment. Ifedi and Okem took my bags inside, and I gestured to Albert to come in.

"No," he said, shaking his head. "I'll see you tomorrow."

"You won't even try the goat meat pepper soup I prepared for you?" my grandmother asked, sounding sorely disappointed.

"No. I have to get home and let Mother know I'm alright. I'm sure she's worried right about now."

"Oh. I understand," my grandmother responded. "Please send my regards to her."

"I will."

My grandmother walked into the house, and I waited behind to wish Albert goodnight. Just before he got in his car, he lowered his head and kissed me lightly on the lips. My heartbeat increased, and a warm feeling swept through my entire frame, leaving me breathless.

"I'll see you tomorrow," he said, as I struggled to avoid his gaze.

"Okay," I whispered.

"Have a good night."

"You too."

I waited until he drove past the gate before I slowly walked into the house, struggling to drag my mind back from the countless thoughts passing through it. I didn't know what to make of the kiss, but I was happy to be home safely with the people I loved. There was no better feeling in the world than that.

* * *

I headed straight for my room, arriving as Okem and Ifedi were just dropping my bags.

"Can you excuse us for a moment?" Okem said to Ifedi.

Ifedi did not immediately oblige his request. At first, she hissed, and with a grimace, she lugged one of my bags on the bed and slowly started taking out one item after another, pulling a chuckle from me.

"Just a moment please," Okem repeated.

"Don't stay too long," she said, when she finally responded. "I also need to spend time with Ona. I haven't seen her in so long. Besides, dinner is ready. Five minutes max!"

I continued to watch the spectacle with amusement. It was unlike Ifedi to be so authoritative, but I guessed she felt it was her right to make sure I wasn't left alone in a room with a man, even if that man was Okem. Who could blame her? She had been with me for so long that at times she forgot I wasn't a small child anymore and didn't need her to protect me.

As soon as she left, Okem pulled me to a corner and looked at me with steely eyes. His Adam's apple bounced up and down as he swallowed a few times.

"What is it?" I asked.

"Are you going to marry that guy?"

"Albert?" I asked, surprised. "I'm not sure. Why do you ask? He hasn't even asked me."

"He hasn't?"

"Well, he has once alluded to that. Something about wanting me by his side. But no. He hasn't asked me."

Okem heaved a sigh of relief.

"Well then. If Albert asks you, will you say yes?" He was staring into my eyes, waiting eagerly for an answer.

I didn't want to deal with the barrage of questions Okem was throwing at me—I was yet to recover from my trip. One part of me wanted to assuage his fears, and another wanted to ask him to leave me alone. He was wearing me out with his questioning, but I chose to take the high road and remain calm.

"Will you say yes?" he repeated, sounding a little defeated this time.

"I don't know," I whined. "I'm not sure. I'll wait till he asks."

"I thought you loved me. Why would you even consider him?"

I had never heard Okem use that word to describe my feelings for him. I know we admired each other very much, and that admiration had changed dramatically over the years. *But love?* Did he really say that? Out loud? I stared at him as a combination of rational and irrational thoughts floated through my head. I had loved Okem like a friend. Indeed, our love had since grown to become so much more. It had grown to something I couldn't explain, and until now, I had never felt pressured to attach a label to it. *What did he expect me to say?* I knew for sure he was trying to force me to decide between him and Albert. I couldn't even decide what dress to wear for a party, or what to eat for dinner—how could I choose between two men?

I looked up a few seconds later, and he was still standing there, willing me to answer. Starting to feel weak in the knees, my heart blurted, *I love you Okem,* though my lips remained shut. I loved him from the bottom of my heart, but I had to be sensible. We were classes apart, and I never imagined that the love I had for him could truly turn into something romantic. He had kissed me once when I was feeling a bit naughty. And I must admit that I felt a little something then. Actually, what I felt was more significant than I described. It was amazing. This happened right before the last semester of school. The kiss had lingered in my mind for months. And since I hadn't imagined that spending my life with him was a practical option, I had brushed it off as quickly as it had happened. My grandmother would never allow me to marry Okem, so why bother? She was already making plans to become in-laws to Albert's parents. It didn't matter to her that Albert hadn't asked me to marry him. She believed the friendship she'd built with his parents over the months was a sign that we were meant for each other.

As I deliberated our plight, Okem grabbed me by the waist and brushed his lips softly against mine before kissing me fervently. I did not have the strength to resist him, so I kissed him back with butterflies in my stomach and light bulbs flashing through my mind. It felt like my head would explode. Nothing could compare to the feelings Okem's kiss erupted in me. It felt magical and out of this world.

He released my waist as we heard a knock on the door, and Ifedi walked in.

"Ifedi," I gasped and looked around for a bit of distraction, anything to hide my embarrassment. I was convinced she could see through me.

"Okay, time is up. Come and eat, both of you," she announced, acting completely oblivious. I wondered if the look on her face was plain pretense or just annoyance. She had a habit of listening through doors, so I didn't doubt she'd been privy to our entire discussion.

We both walked silently behind her like two lambs to the slaughter. As soon as we were out of the room, I glanced at Okem. The look on his face was a combination of triumph and euphoria.

CHAPTER EIGHT

I **CONTINUED TO** see Albert during that break, although I couldn't quell thoughts of Okem—a consequence of our most recent kiss. The kiss opened my eyes to my true feelings for him—feelings that continued to grow to the point that he occupied both my waking and sleeping thoughts. I was miserable and confused with Okem constantly on my mind. Anyone could see that whatever was bothering me affected the progress of my relationship with Albert. After Ifedi commented on my dilly-dallying between two men, I started to avoid Okem to allow room for my relationship with Albert to grow. Since my relationship with Albert was still the more practical option, it provided me with the justification I needed to erase the feelings of guilt that were cropping up in my head because of how I treated Okem. Soon, I began to anticipate the comfort a marriage to Albert would afford me. But that didn't reduce the pain I felt from missing Okem. Until that kiss, I had never seen Okem as more than a best friend. Well, who was I kidding? The truth was that for a while, Okem and I had been inseparable, and everyone who knew us could tell that from a mile away.

Albert always hated my relationship with Okem. He couldn't understand why despite the difference in our status, our bond of friendship was stronger than any he'd ever seen. He could feel Okem's love for me. I could tell from his jealous tantrums. What I couldn't imagine was how he would feel if he understood the depth of my own feelings for Okem.

* * *

Two weeks into my holiday, Okem marched towards me while I was curled up on the sofa in the parlor.

"I'm tired of you ignoring me," he said in a baritone, a dull expression clouding his perfectly sculpted face.

"How did you come to the conclusion that I was ignoring you?" I'd asked, rolling my eyes.

"I just know. Anyway, I came to tell you that I'm leaving home."

Instantly, my nonchalance turned to fear, my thoughts flew in every direction, and my heart almost rushed into my mouth. I hated to imagine what would happen if Okem followed through with his threat.

"Where will you go?" I asked.

"I don't know. Anywhere but here."

"You shouldn't. This is your home," I retorted, trying hard to hide my discomfort. "My grandma will be devastated."

"What about you? Will you be devastated?"

I turned my head away from him and looked into the distance.

"Will you?" he repeated. "You can't even give me a straight answer."

"Don't go, Okem," I blurted.

"I have to. I can't bear the thought of you marrying that guy. I have to go out there and try to create something I can be proud of."

"Why? Okem Don't go," I pleaded. "I'll—"

"You'll what?" he asked, kneeling before me and looking up to my forlorn face. "Will you miss me? Come with me."

My heart was in my mouth, and I realized I couldn't let him go. At the sound of the doorbell, he sprung to his feet and walked out of the room. Ifedi appeared out of nowhere to get the door. I shook my head in confusion just as Albert walked in.

"Did I meet you at a bad time?" Albert asked.

"No," I lied, staring out of the window, my blank eyes not really seeing the beautiful garden within my view.

Albert took my hand and led me to my grandfather's study.

"It doesn't seem like nothing," he said. "You seem terribly upset. Hey, I have some news for you. Maybe that will cheer you up. I'll be joining father next month in his business in Ide. I decided to stay home rather than constantly shuttling back and forth to Ajidi. That's how much I want to be near you."

I smiled through pursed lips. *At least someone is staying*, I thought to myself.

"Are you happy about the news?" Albert asked.

"I'm happy," I said, looking into his eyes, and forcing another smile.

"You don't look at all happy."

"I'm just feeling tired."

"Sorry to hear that. There's something I've been meaning to ask you, but I wanted to wait until I had concluded this business matter with my father. Now, there's no reason for me to wait any longer."

My heart fluttered. I thought I knew what this was all about, but I couldn't be so sure. I heard Ifedi skittering around the door, and when I turned, she acted as though she was searching for something and then left soon after. Albert grabbed the handle and gently closed the door, but I was sure Ifedi had her ear pressed against the wall, waiting to hear what Albert was about to say.

"Will you marry me, Ona?" Albert asked after a few seconds had elapsed.

I was sort of expecting him to ask me, but I was still stunned by his directness.

"You don't have to answer now," he declared before I had time to speak. "Think about it and let me know tomorrow."

"Tomorrow?" I said, a little discomfort seeping through my tone.

"Take some time to think about it and let me know. When I see you're ready, I'll make a formal proposal, until then just know that I want to spend the rest of my life with you."

I loved Albert, but I didn't think I could say anything to him until I had sorted out my feelings for Okem.

* * *

After Albert left, I stood still pondering everything that had just happened. A few minutes later, Ifedi rushed into the study with a sheepish grin on her face.

"Do you love him then? Will you marry him?" she asked.

I stared at her and refused to respond.

A moment passed before she asked another question.

"What about Okem?"

"Okem? What about him?" I eyed her furtively.

"Do you love him? Will you marry him if he asks?"

"Hmm... marriage? I haven't thought about that. I don't know how people will feel about me marrying someone of a lower status than me. They will think I have no taste. They will castigate me and wonder why I gave up comfort for... did you hear that?"

I shot up as I heard a rustle behind the door.

"Go on," Ifedi urged me.

"What was that? I could have sworn something moved behind that door."

"It could be the servant setting dinner. Don't worry about it. What were you saying? Do you prefer Albert, then?"

"No. Despite that little hitch and the fact that I have to convince my grandmother to let me marry Okem, I don't think there's any other person on this earth for me besides him."

"Really?" She asked wide-eyed.

I nodded, my gaze absently wandering all over her face.

"How can you say that? Albert is more than suitable. What is wrong with you Ona? Why can't you make a simple rational decision? You're not a child anymore."

As she spoke, my mind floated between Okem and Albert before an uneasy feeling overcame me, and I sighed to release the pent up emotion.

"What?" she continued, shaking her head fiercely. "What do you have to say about what I just told you?"

"I agree. Albert is wonderful, but I've just realized Okem is my soul mate!"

My eyes welled up with tears the moment I said those words.

"Really?" Ifedi shrieked, looking around as though seeking confirmation for what she had just heard.

"Yes! He's the one I want to come home to every night. I want to tell him all my secrets, and I want to bear all his children…a dozen, if God will allow me." I stopped and put my hands on my chest to control the heaving as I came to that final realization. "Okem is the one I love. It's always been Okem. He doesn't have to leave after all. And if he insists, I'll just go with him. I'll head down to his room right now and tell him how I feel."

Ifedi's jaw dropped as I pranced out of the room following my announcement.

I ran past the living room and through the entire hallway to Okem's bedroom at the north end of the house overlooking the yard where the gardener reared his goats. As I approached, I called his name, "Okem… Okem," as I usually did. Most times, he would abandon what he was doing and run down the hall when he heard me approaching, but all I heard this time were echoes of my voice, and then silence. When I got closer, the door to his room was slightly open. I looked inside and his bed was bare. I looked around the room; it was stripped of any sign of life.

When I looked behind me, Ifedi seemed just as stunned as I was as she stared at the empty room.

"What happened?" I asked Ifedi, as though she must know.

She shook her head twice. "He must have heard you."

"What?"

"I don't know," she said demurely, throwing her hands up in the air. "He was... He must have been listening at the door."

"And so what? I said he was my world."

I was trembling and gasping for air. Tears stung my eyes and rolled down my cheeks while I stumbled towards his bed and plopped down. "I said he was my soul mate," I repeated, grabbing my stomach.

"I don't think he heard that part. If you recall, we heard the rustle behind the door after you said he belonged to a different class. He must have left then."

"What?" I screeched.

I felt as though someone had taken a dagger and pushed it into my heart. The pain was deeper than anything I had ever felt in my lifetime. It was deeper than the pain I felt when my parents forced me to move in with my grandparents. It was even deeper than the pain of when my grandfather left our world. Everything seemed to be at a standstill. No movement from the leaves on the mango trees outside, even with the heavy wind. No movement from Ifedi, who always knew how to calm me down. No movement from the birds who had been fluttering outside the window just a moment ago and no flutter at the gate to indicate Okem's return. It was as though the entire world had frozen because my own heart had grown cold.

* * *

"Papa," I said aloud, collapsing on the sofa in tears as I recalled what my grandfather had said the last time I was in Luenah. The ache in my heart convinced me I had surrendered something significant. It all became clear to me. Everything did. My grandfather had said that I needed to exchange something. I felt I did that tonight.

My distress drove me to Luenah. I found myself walking down the narrow path with one foot in front of the other. Out on the seashore, the atmosphere was dreary, and the skies were dark. So dark, not a single star danced in it. I could hardly remember a time I'd viewed Luenah in such a state. I had been under the impression that nighttime didn't exist there. I sat down to rest, as my mind processed a series of thoughts. The sand was cold against my skin. I closed my eyes and let the wind blow over my face, carrying with it scents of seaweed and brine. There was no sound, but I knew he had come when he tapped my shoulder and sat next to me.

"Yes?" my grandfather responded.

"Papa, did I do the right thing?" I sobbed.

"What does your heart tell you?"

I cried some more. "I don't know."

"I'm sure you know enough now about finding your purpose to recognize that the person you plan to spend your life with plays a big role in achieving it."

I looked at him with wet eyes.

"Who is the right person?"

"That's your choice to make."

"What do I do now?"

The exchange is yours. If you choose the wrong person, you may wander around this earth searching non-stop for your purpose. Should you find it, the wrong person will thwart its fulfillment. Your exchange is your opportunity cost. It is what you give up for choosing one option over the other. But beyond that, it is what you're unwilling to bear at the point of making a choice, which is what makes it so difficult to fathom."

I wiped my face to dry the tears coursing down my cheeks as I tried to make sense of his words. "I wonder why being an *Eri*, I'm still susceptible to this much pain."

"The gift is not self-serving. Rather, it's meant for the service of others."

"I understand... What's happening here?" I said, pointing to the sky. "It's never been this dark in Luenah."

"There are so many things you're yet to—"

He barely mouthed the next word before he

vanished. I came out of Luenah as quickly as I had entered. Ifedi had been watching me the entire time I was there. I didn't think I stayed too long, which was a good thing; otherwise, she would have panicked and called my grandmother. Her reaction told me she had gotten used to my *fainting episodes*, her label for my trips to Luenah.

"How long was I out?"

"Two seconds. You sound as though this nonsense is normal. We need to check you into a hospital the next time it happens."

I ignored her as I recalled what drove me to Luenah in the first place. Okem had overheard me. Had I mastered the lesson about the exchange earlier, I would not have said those mean words that sent him away. I wouldn't have even bothered about his status and class. I had failed to make the exchange that was required of me. The one I knew was right for me. I gave up love for what I thought would bring me happiness—the security a life with Albert would provide. This was exactly what my grandfather had warned me against.

"Is Okem really gone," I asked Ifedi.

"We could still bring him back," she said rather unconvincingly.

"How could he leave without telling me?"

She shrugged.

"I don't know."

"Why does love hurt so much?" I moaned,

shaking my head from side to side.

* * *

As I began to get accustomed to the possibility that I may never see Okem again, we heard the rattling sound of the wrought iron gate. I looked at Ifedi expectantly, with the last shred of hope that Okem may have returned. We ran out of the room and got on the porch as the gardener was starting downhill, picking up speed as he rode towards the main house. I burst into tears again and immediately stepped down to meet him.

"Where's Okem?" I asked.

"I dropped him at the bus stop," he said after a slight hesitation.

"Do you know where he was going? Did he say?"

The gardener shook his head slowly.

"Ona, come," Ifedi said, grabbing me by my hand.

"Come where? Leave me alone," I screamed at Ifedi, causing her to jump.

"Come."

I swallowed hard as my heart skipped a beat, and I gasped for air, collapsing into Ifedi's arms.

"He'll come back," Ifedi said. "He'll be back before dawn. He loves you too much. He always comes back."

CHAPTER NINE

OKEM DIDN'T COME back by dawn as Ifedi had predicted. Albert returned the following day to enquire about his proposal. I was hiding in my room, drowning in my misery, when Ifedi rushed in to offer some help.

"You can't meet him looking like that," she griped, pointing at my matted hair, evidence of my self-neglect.

"Like how?" I had asked. "I can't meet him at all. What will I say to him? What will he think of me? Besides, I don't care to see anyone right now. Don't make me do this, Ifedi. Please don't."

"Sit down," she ordered, pointing at a chair, and ignoring my pleas.

I felt like a little girl all over again and did as she asked. I was too weak to fight Ifedi. In my state, she could have ordered me to the ends of the earth, and I would still have obeyed her. She entered the bathroom and returned with a cup of water. With one hand, she poured the water on the ends of my hair, and with the other, she separated the chunks of hair. To detangle, she combed through the tresses, starting from the tips and making her way down to the roots, yanking my skull back and forth in the process. I jerked as she pulled my hair a tad too heavily and tapped me hard on the shoulder with the comb, hitting my clavicle.

"Stop!" I shouted, causing her to jump. "Why did you do that?"

"I've asked you so many times to sit still while I'm plaiting your hair."

"It's not funny, Ifedi. The next time you hit me like that, I'll hit you right back."

"Sorry," she said in a drawn voice. "I was just playing with you. You've been too morose these days. I wanted to wake you up."

"And so what? Don't play like that. I don't like it."

"I've said sorry. How are things with Albert?"

"So-so."

"What does that mean?"

"How will I know? I'll have to wait until I see him. I just hope I can look him straight in the eye after what happened yesterday."

"I agree, and I hope you'll do the right thing this

time. You can go now," she continued, tapping me again, gently this time. If you play your cards right, you just might be our next queen."

"Haha," I responded dryly.

Albert had been waiting nearly an hour by the time I got downstairs. He came towards me and reached out for a hug, but I retreated slowly from his embrace and took the seat next to him.

"What's wrong?" he asked, a sullen expression crossing his face.

"Nothing. I've been feeling a little sick lately."

"You mentioned you were tired yesterday. Why don't you let me take you to a doctor?"

"No. It's not that kind of sickness. I'll be fine after I rest for a day or two."

"I hope so. What about my proposal? Have you had time to think about it? Will you marry me or not?"

"I don't know. Not now," I said beseechingly.

"Not now? When then? Could... Could you at least give me an idea of when I can expect an answer?"

"Albert, I said I don't know," I reiterated, sighing deeply. "Can you leave now? I need to head back to my room and finish something."

I couldn't possibly tell him right then that Okem was the one I wanted, not him. That would break his heart into so many pieces it would be impossible to put them back together.

"Ona, I honestly can't fathom the reason for your change in attitude. I just can't!" he said, getting up and leaving in annoyance, causing me further dejection.

* * *

That night, I dreamt that as I was walking down a path, a creature strode right past me, causing a slight tremor on the ground. As I was trying to regain my balance, it crept behind a shrub and glared at me with huge, glowing eyes, frightening me. I had woken suddenly from the nightmare and was sweating profusely. I could have sworn the face on the creature was of someone I knew very well, but I couldn't say who it was with certainty.

In the morning, as I reflected on the meaning of my dream and wondering if it had something to do with Okem's disappearance or even with the darkness I experienced the last time I was in Luenah, Ifedi rushed into my room wearing a sullen look on her face.

"Ona, there's something I think you should know," she said, sitting slowly by my bedside.

"Is Okem back?" I asked excitedly, pushing the covers away and scrambling to the other side of the bed to get up without obstruction.

"Ona, no. Okem is not back. And I don't think you should keep torturing yourself because of Okem."

"What do you mean?" I was angry that Ifedi did not understand the amount of pain Okem's disappearance caused me.

"I'm sorry," she said. "Even more so for what I'm about to tell you. Honestly, if I had known it would have caused you such grief, I wouldn't have agreed to the plot."

"Stop talking in riddles. Tell me what you want to say."

"Okem asked me to pose those questions to you after we both overheard Albert propose."

"I don't understand," I said, shaking my head non-stop while I waited for her to explain.

"I refused at first, but he begged me. He wanted to hear for himself who you would choose, him or Albert. I don't think it ever crossed his mind that you would pick anyone else over him—"

"Wait! You're saying Okem set all that up to figure out who I wanted between him and Albert?"

She nodded.

"I didn't know—"

"How could you have agreed to such a thing?" I yelled, stopping her mid-sentence. "And why did you not alert me when I was saying those horrible things about him? Why?"

I pulled off the covers completely and paced the room angrily, shaking my head in disdain. Stopping at the window, a ray of the morning sun reminded me that I hadn't experienced joy in a while.

"Ona, it didn't occur to me at the time that you liked Okem this much. And what was I to do? It seemed to me that you really liked Albert too. Don't blame me."

"Well, it's not your fault. His plan worked. He got the answers he needed for his burning questions and got burned in the end. If only he wasn't so cocky and impatient, he would have waited to hear me out!" I was fuming, staring out the window but only seeing red.

"Okem was a hundred percent sure you would choose him," Ifedi said. "He kept saying that your constant rejection was your way of testing his patience."

"He said that?" I shrieked, turning around to look at Ifedi.

"Yes, he did."

"Oh, God! He really thinks everything is about him. Does he think I play games like that?"

Ifedi rose from her position on the bed and grabbed my shoulders. She dragged me away from the window and gently guided me to the settee.

"What should I do now?" I sobbed, looking down in embarrassment.

I was angry at Okem, but he wasn't there for me to take my anger out on him. I was even angrier at Ifedi for agreeing to such foolery, but I needed her to comfort me. Regardless, it felt like a betrayal. I raised my head to look at her face. At that moment, I remembered my nightmare from the night before, and it occurred to me hers was the face I saw looking at me through the shrubbery, and I shuddered.

* * *

At school, I thought endlessly about Okem, walking around with the aftermath of many sleepless nights and a heavy heart. I saw him everywhere I looked and I refused to eat.

The situation went from bad to worse on my way to a lecture on a very hot afternoon. A faint buzzing in my ears stopped me in my tracks, and I almost fainted on the stairs as a throng of students sped by to get to class on time. Luckily, a good samaritan stopped and helped me regain my balance before taking me to the clinic. The next day, my grandmother rode for six hours from Ntebe to Ajidi to speak to me after dissuading my mother from abandoning an important assignment to be by my side.

Her words got through to me. After that day, I vowed to turn things around, but it wasn't easy. I sought every possible way to render Okem insignificant in my life. A shift occurred in my consciousness. My grief evolved. From crying and mourning, I became blinded by hatred. I hated Okem so much that whenever I thought about him, I imagined an egocentric maniac. It made me feel better, but only briefly. Over time, even though I still thought about him every day, I started to feel like my old self again.

From hatred, I developed a genuine concern for him. I believed it was stupid of me to have ignored and avoided him after Albert and I became close. It was even more stupid of me to say those things about him. But I didn't just blame myself. I blamed Okem too. If only he had been patient enough to hear my true feelings. If only he had trusted enough in the love we had for each other. If only he had a stronger backbone. So many ifs. We were both responsible.

CHAPTER TEN

"**I KNOW WHY** Ona seemed so out of sorts a while ago," Albert had said to my grandmother during a visit a year after Okem's disappearance.

"Why?" she asked, panic-stricken that my indecision had become public knowledge and that my chances of marrying the most eligible bachelor in Ide and environs had been completely dashed.

"Depression," he'd answered. "What else? It happens to the best of us."

"Oh," my grandmother said with relief.

I could see the smile spreading over her entire face as she leaned into the chair.

Hilarious. It was depression, alright. Albert, I believed, knew the cause of my problem and was only pretending in hopes that someday I would get over whatever it was and realize I was in love with him. It must have been clear to him as it was to everyone else that my unhappiness started right after Okem unexpectedly disappeared, but he still insisted on marrying me under those circumstances. I had spared him the details of my troubles in fear that I would hurt him and possibly lose him. And I was just too ashamed to discuss the topic with him. Too ashamed to reveal to him that I was mourning the rejection from the person he once referred to as "servant boy."

My caution with Albert wasn't solely to preserve my chance of marrying the most eligible bachelor. That was my grandmother's goal. What no one else knew was that I had started developing some affection for him over the past few months. Albert had slowly found his way through the crevices Okem left in my heart and filled the spaces with his strength and assurance. He showed me what it was like to be loved despite my unwillingness to reciprocate such love. With time I started to believe I was capable of loving him as much as he loved me. It could end up being that Albert was meant for me. My grandfather hadn't told me which choice was right. He had left the task of choosing to me. "Choosing for you would tip the balance in the universe," he had said. The school of life, he called it. I had been provided the lesson. Now it was up to me to make my own choices and learn from any mistakes along the way.

* * *

Despite my progress and Albert's efforts to keep me happy, I still slipped in and out of a low mood occasionally. One afternoon, my heart was heavy, and my hand was clenched around the lower part of my stomach as I looked out of the window while droplets of rain fell from the sky. The ravine from my window looked so lush and beautiful; it seemed to me Okem might be hiding there for a moment. I thought I'd seen something, so I moved closer to get a better look.

"Are you still thinking about that boy?" Ifedi asked, startling me.

I hadn't heard her enter the room.

"No," I said, shaking my head.

Her question had worsened my emotional state and caused my eyes to water profusely. I thought I had shed every single tear in me. In the past few months, they had rolled down my cheeks like rainwater rolling down corrugated iron sheets and splattered on the ground all around me. I remained crouched on the chair, looking out the window. Ifedi came closer and sat right beside me. I could see the pain in her expression as she gently wiped my cheeks. She didn't say another word, letting us sit in silence, which I was grateful for.

"How could Okem stay away for so long?" I finally said, looking at her with forlorn eyes.

Ifedi looked at me blankly while she waited for me to calm down. Too ashamed to look in her direction, I placed my head between my knees, but she reached for my chin and raised it to glare at me.

"You need to learn to let go," she finally said after a few seconds had passed.

I shut my swollen eyes to get rid of the buildup of tears.

"That's what I've been trying to do," I said after I opened my eyes again.

"You're doing a poor job at it."

"How?"

"I'm glad you asked," she said, kneeling before me and taking both of my hands in hers. "Listen carefully," she said.

"I am listening," I said, waiting eagerly for her to begin.

"No. Look at me. Not like Ifedi, your friend or companion, or whatever else you see me as now. Really look at me."

"Yes, I'm looking at you."

I sniffed and took a good look at her. The creases and lines around her mouth told the story of the thirty-five years she'd spent on this earth. There was sadness—deep sadness—in her eyes. My apprehension increased the longer I looked at her, so I sighed and tried to look away.

"What do you see?" she asked, dragging my chin to continue facing her.

"I don't know," I gasped in protest. "Stop acting as if I'm just seeing you for the first time. You look a little tired. Leave me alone. I need to rest."

Taken aback, she released my chin but ignored my comment.

"I'm sorry, Ifedi. I didn't mean to hurt you."

"Do you think this is the life I wanted for myself? Before you respond, I'll first say that I have no regrets. I have worked for you for several years now. If you recall, I was barely an adult when I came to live with you and your grandparents. I loved you from the moment I set my eyes on you, but what you don't know is that I too had hopes and dreams of my own. I was even in love at one point."

"What happened? Where is he?" I asked wondering how I had been oblivious to the fact that Ifedi had been in love. For some reason, the prospect that Ifedi had ever been in love made my sorrows disappear. I slumped back into my chair when I realized my questions had turned her tired eyes a bit teary. It was the first time I'd ever seen Ifedi cry. It broke my heart.

"I don't know where he is now," she finally said. "But I dream of him every day. I imagine that he is mine and that we're here together. We have children running around the house, making a mess, and I don't mind because I'm happy—too happy to care. And it's all in here," she said, placing a hand on her chest.

"Why?" I asked. "Why don't you just go after him?"

"Why haven't you gone after Okem?"

I stared at her in disbelief.

"I don't know where he is."

"Exactly! I also don't know where this man I talk about is. He could be dead; I don't know. He could even be married with children."

"Then why do you keep dreaming about him?"

"It makes me happy," she said, getting up and walking towards the window. "Otherwise, I would be crying just like you."

"Like me? That's not fair."

The rain had turned into a slight drizzle and taken along with it the tears in my eyes.

Ifedi turned to me and spoke with authority. "If you love Okem, replace your dejection with dreaming. You will see how much better that will make you feel. Dreaming helps keep hope alive, hope for the future. It's a way for you to let go without feeling as though you're betraying him."

"I don't think it's as easy as you make it sound."

"What do you have to lose? Try it."

From that day, I dreamed instead of crying. I dreamed that Okem was back, and we got married in a lavish ceremony, and we had children and that we lived to a ripe old age. My dreams replaced the dejection I felt. I slowly recovered and became happy again. I was to graduate by the end of that year, and my grandmother organized a huge party. Albert asked me to marry him again at that party, and I said yes. Albert loved me, so it was easy. I still hoped Okem would be back, and I still dreamed about him occasionally, but I loved Albert in a different way, and I was willing to make it work. Besides, no one had heard from Okem since he left. Everyone wondered if he was still alive. I wondered if he would ever come back to Ntebe.

* * *

Months of intense grooming at the palace in Ide followed my betrothal to Albert. It was necessary for me to become the wife of the future King. A driver picked me up daily from Ntebe and drove me to Ide for the exercise. The process included training on etiquette and ethics suitable for a queen. We carried out several traditional rites, some of which made me uncomfortable, but I brushed them off as necessary for a future queen. It was not until I complained to my grandmother that she made everything clear. After a day of intense training in Ide, I sat down in her room and asked her what I'd been meaning to for a while.

"Why do I have to learn so much? I don't even think Albert is going through as much as I have to, and he is to be king, not me."

"How do you know he's not going through worse? You don't attend his sessions with him."

"I know that he is undergoing less torture for a fact. Do you see all they've put me through? I did not ask for this."

"Listen, dear. When you finally get married, your husband will be the head. You will be the neck. As the neck, your role is as important as that of the head, even likely more important than his because no matter what the head wants to do, the neck will have to approve as the former could not possibly move without the latter."

"But what if I ruin everything?" I asked after a moment's pause.

"You cannot run away from your calling. This is what you have been called to do. You tried to run away once and got pulled back by providence. The same providence will keep restricting you no matter how hard you try, so you need to let it take its course."

I wondered what my grandmother meant by "you tried once." I was sure she was referring to Okem, but I was afraid to probe as I didn't want to open up a can of worms. She had sounded like my grandfather when she talked about my calling. I wondered if she had been talking to him too. If so, they had both succeeded in confusing me further. Unlike her, though, my grandfather had refused to assist me with making choices.

"What are you referring to, Mama?" I asked, seizing the opportunity to grill her further about my calling. "I see no way the things they're forcing me to learn will help me achieve my goals. None of the things they're stuffing down my throat includes any of my wishes."

"What are your wishes," she asked, ignoring my tantrum.

"Papa had said—"

She hummed and flapped her wrapper on her thighs at the mere mention of Papa, which didn't surprise me. She never liked speaking about my grandfather. His death had been so painful to her, she shut down anytime anyone or anything reminded her of him. The first time I met him in Luenah, I had guarded the meeting jealously. It was my secret. As time passed, and I noticed my grandmother wouldn't entertain any talk of him, I realized I didn't need to worry about her probing and discovering my secret.

"Your wishes?" she repeated. "What things do you wish for in this life?"

"I just want to be loved, to answer my call of duty, and to find happiness."

"Don't you think this is your call of duty then?"

"I don't know."

I was thinking about Okem at that moment, but I couldn't tell her that. Although I was set on marrying Albert, I was still in love with Okem. As Okem's wife, I was pretty sure I would have had to answer to a different call of duty, working as a government lawyer or running my own law firm, so how could I respond to my grandmother's question without addressing that aspect? So far, I was yet to conquer love. Duty had been decided for me, as a consequence of the love 'I chose.'

"My dear, everything you're going through is preparing you for what you were meant to be," she said, interrupting my reverie. "Have you ever heard the saying, *man proposes and God disposes*? If you believe, fate will always drive you through the required tests and supply you with the wisdom you need to achieve your purpose. In the end, you will have acquired all the knowledge required to do something bigger than yourself. Something you could never have imagined. No matter how hard you try to conquer love and duty, or even achieve happiness, if you're not living your purpose, you will never be fulfilled. And if you're not fulfilled, you can never claim to have found happiness."

"What if I marry the wrong person? Will I still be able to achieve my purpose?"

She hummed and shook her head.

"What then?" I asked, glaring at her.

"It will be very difficult. Almost impossible," she finally said. "Marrying the wrong person can send your entire life down the drain." She paused and stuck her neck out for emphasis. "You will marry the person who will help you achieve your purpose, and you will help him with his, in return. Don't worry so much. I believe you're on the right track. Everything happens for a reason; everything will eventually align for your good. Believe that God is love, and he will bring forth all you need. He will."

"You think so?"

"I know so. Ever since you were a little girl, you've talked about lessening the plight of the less privileged. Becoming Queen seems to be a great way for you to do that."

"You're right, Grandma. This is my chance to do something for the greater good. I can't think of a better way. I'll influence policy, laws, judgments, and even the economy."

"There you go! I always thought you were a queen at heart. You seem truly energized now."

She was right. I could feel the excitement too. It was bubbling right in my core.

Though I still yearned for Okem, I heeded my grandmother's advice and prepared for my marriage to the Crown Prince.

CHAPTER ELEVEN

WE CELEBRATED OUR engagement in a lavish ceremony that attracted countless dignitaries from near and far. Amidst the crowds, I counted at least seven governors and two former presidents. Security personnel and soldiers with armored vehicles lined the roads from Ide to Ntebe. All the shops were closed, and the major roads were blocked off to control traffic. For the first time, I got a glimpse of the significance of my position. Countless times, I was told of how beautiful I looked in my wedding attire. After many days of searching for the ideal fabric, my grandmother finally came across the perfect one for my attire—a beautiful *asooke* in wine red and gold. She had it custom embroidered to ensure it was one-of-a-kind.

Amah and nine other friends, wearing a

glamorous, green and gold embroidered *aso-ebi* uniform escorted me as I made my entrance at the ceremony. Our clothes and our faces glistened from the lights emanating from the intricately designed lamps. They were strategically positioned outside to create a striking ambiance with the landscape and the structures that once awed me as a kid. When I got older, those structures had begun to lose their significance, but that night, they stood out and reminded me what a magnificent home my grandfather's was.

The heavens were magnificent, too. A half-moon danced in the sky, radiant against a dark background completely rid of stars. Both families were seated on opposite sides of each other while the traditional rites were carried out. I was taken through a test—a question-and-answer section by the patriarch of Albert's family to confirm that I had been properly groomed for my position. I answered everything correctly and was taken before my family, my grandmother, mother, and father, as well as my aunties and uncles. They whispered words of advice to me as I stooped before each one of them. I was then guided by my 'ladies in waiting' to Albert's family so they could also offer their blessings to me. After they muttered incantations to welcome me to the family, I was asked to kneel before Albert. He placed his hand on my back and said a prayer and a loud, "Amen," to which the crowd responded in unison with a reverberating, "Amen!"

Next, Albert took my hands and guided me to the seat beside his. The gesture reminded me of the years I spent sitting next to Papa, and a feeling of déjà vu swept over me. I couldn't help but wonder how this memorable day would have been different if my life had taken another path. Had my betrothed been Okem, I would no doubt be looking at a completely different sea of faces, beaming with joy and laughter. Friends, family, and neighbors with no other motive than to have a good time would have filled the seats. The pomp and pageantry would be at a bare minimum, and there would be no politics, no hierarchy, and no us and them.

"Ona, Ona," I felt someone calling and forcing me out of my reverie.

Albert was smiling down at me. Squeezing my hand firmly, he whispered, "My Queen."

I blinked and looked at him inquisitively. Calling me by my future title had startled me and reminded me of what I was destined to do; to marry Albert and be his Queen. He chuckled at my reaction.

"You better get used to it, my darling," he said before I could respond.

"Ye—yes," I stuttered.

I loved Albert for what he was, prim and proper and almost impenetrable, and he loved me—although more than I loved him. He worshipped the ground I walked on and was always at my beck and call. He bought me gifts almost daily. But he was rich so buying gifts for me didn't require any sacrifice on his part. He didn't get additional points for that. For all his other qualities, he was perfect for me as my grandmother had insinuated. I hoped and prayed as I sat next to him that Okem would soon become a passing memory. A dream. One filled with enough hope to help me achieve the balance I so desperately sought.

The ceremony continued with eating and dancing. Albert and I performed our first dance amidst cheers from the crowd. Wads of money in different currencies were sprayed all over us by the guests as we entertained them with our unrehearsed dance moves. The staff assigned to pick up the cash tripped over each other as the pieces flew in every direction while the guests tried to outdo one another in their display of riches. It was hard for me to imagine how the actual wedding would be if the engagement ceremony alone could garner such attention. I knew it was a big deal to be affianced to the future King, but there was no way I could have anticipated the grandeur and glory with which the ceremony was carried out.

It was long past midnight before the last guest left. I remained in our home in Ntebe, where I was expected to live until after our wedding in two months. Albert couldn't wait. His excitement was unmistakable at the ceremony. He told anyone who cared to listen how eager he was for me to become his wife and move in with him.

Though we didn't live together, we began to spend more time together and got closer in subsequent weeks. I visited Ide more often but never spent the night there except during important occasions—weddings or cultural celebrations. In those instances, a separate room, decorated as fit for a princess, was always reserved for me.

* * *

I relaxed into my new routine with Albert, although I still thought about Okem once in a while. One Saturday morning after Albert came to visit me in Ntebe, I casually brought up the subject of Okem as we stood side-by-side on the porch.

"I wonder what became of Okem. He just disappeared into thin air, and no one has seen him since then."

Albert crossed his hands and leaned back against the post.

"I sent a delegate to search for him some time ago," he said after a moment's pause.

"Really? When? I didn't know that." I said excitedly, making a slight half-turn to look at him.

For a moment, his gaze strolled absently over my face before he asked, "Why does that excite you so much?"

"I don't know," I said, slightly embarrassed. "I

just didn't think you cared what happened to him."

"He was like your best friend. Why shouldn't I care?"

"Well, thank you," I responded, despite sensing a dose of sarcasm from him.

"You're welcome."

"Any word at all from your search?" I asked, trying my best to remain composed.

He was silent for a moment before frowning and shaking his head.

"No word," he responded, returning to his original position.

* * *

I settled into my role as the future wife of the future King. As we prepared for our wedding, Albert's team bore the brunt of the work. I helped as much as I could and even suggested for my grandmother's address—my address—to be used for some of the correspondence just to spread the risk. RSVPs for some of his closest friends came to me. Together, Ifedi and I sorted through the mail daily, recorded the responses, and then handed them to him whenever he came by.

As the wedding drew closer, Albert showed himself to be a wonderful partner. Being so kind and considerate, he checked in every day to see how things were going, but my mind still wandered, as usual. If not on Okem or my adventures in Luenah, it was on the unending steps we needed to complete for the wedding. I caught Albert looking at me at times and shaking his head whenever I stepped into a reverie. I talked to him about Okem one more time to see if I could find out more about the search he had carried out to find him. This time around, he provided vague answers and changed the topic.

His reluctance deterred me from asking any further. I didn't want to reveal how much Okem's disappearance affected me. My love for Okem was still alive, but it was not immediately apparent. It existed in my dreams and in the innermost crevices of my heart where no one could reach for it without first prying me open. It was safe.

* * *

"As the wedding planning intensifies, I find myself thinking more and more about Okem," I said to Amah one sunny afternoon when she came to visit. She came by often to assist me with wedding preparations while she waited for her applications to a Master's Program to come through.

"In what sense?" she asked, raising her brows as she stepped forward to sit beside me on the bed. As she waited for me to respond, she crossed her legs and adjusted her back to face me directly.

"Oh. It's not what you think," I said, waving my hand abruptly. "Albert had been searching for him, and he claims there's no word on his whereabouts—"

"Is that a fact? Albert was searching for Okem?" she asked, wide-eyed.

"He told me so himself, which surprised me. I always thought Okem infuriated him."

"*Hmm!* Then leave it alone and focus on Albert. I can't believe soon you'll be the Queen of Ide. Will I have to bow to you then?" She asked with a disapproving look."

"You don't have to bow to me, but you can feed me grapes," I responded, winking and pulling a long hiss from her.

"In your dreams."

"But on a serious note," I continued. "I can't pretend Okem never existed after my conversation with Albert. What if Okem is in danger? We are all he has after all."

"You make a good point. And you say Albert has found nothing?"

"Nothing so far."

"That's serious then, Ona. Knowing Albert, he would have used the best available resource for his search. If that did not produce any results, then Okem must be seriously lost. In that case, it's your responsibility to find him."

I sat upright to improve my focus as I came to the sudden realization that I may have neglected my responsibility towards Okem.

"I'll ask Albert again," I said, trying my best to sound calmer than I was feeling. "The problem is, he shuts down whenever I bring up Okem. I'll try again, though."

Amah shook her head. "Albert may not be your best bet, for obvious reasons. If this is so important to you, I'd say you should try to find Okem on your own."

"When he first disappeared, I actually thought about hiring a private investigator to look for him," I confided.

"*Hian!*" Amah exclaimed. "Do you think we're in a Hollywood movie? Which money would you have used then to hire a private investigator? You were still a student when Okem left. And since graduating, you've proudly refused to accept any pocket money from your parents. To add to that, you're not working yet, and you don't get an income until you resume your new role, and even then, *e get as e be.*"

"I have some money set aside. I don't think it's a big deal."

"Save your money for a rainy day. I can ask my Uncle in Ajidi to help. He can ask the Ntebe people there if anyone has heard of Okem. Believe me, I'm sure he's hiding somewhere in Ajidi. That's where all the runaways go."

"Don't talk about Okem like that," I chided.

"Okay *o,*" she said, shrugging her shoulders. "Seriously, my uncle is your best bet. Do you have a picture of Okem? I can send it to him, and he can contact you directly if he finds anything since I may soon be leaving for London."

"Thank you so much Amah. I'd really appreciate that. *Hmm!* With all this talk about London, I hope you'll be around for the wedding."

"You should know by now that I wouldn't miss it for the world," she said with a smirk.

"I believe you, but make sure you get someone before you leave," I teased.

"Why do I need to?" she scoffed. "There are many fishes in the part of the Atlantic that crosses the United Kingdom."

"But your parents will like you to marry an Ntebe man. What about that boy you're seeing? The one that just moved back from the states?"

Amah chuckled.

"That one? Do you know what he said to me the other day?"

"What?" I asked, adjusting myself on the bed.

"That if I like we can do it."

"Do what?" I asked, laughing and pounding my fists on the pillow when I finally understood what she meant. "Amah, please don't kill me!"

"*Ehen.* That's the one you want me to stake my life on. Please, I want a prince like Albert. I'm sure Albert doesn't ask you to 'do it.' If he did, I'd have known by now."

* * *

Amah kept her end of the bargain and contacted her Uncle in Ajidi on my behalf. He sent me updates at intervals, but the search revealed nothing for weeks. The last time I heard from him, he had concluded that Okem could not be in Ajidi at all. The other alternative he offered was that he had either changed his name to stay anonymous or had died a while ago. I refused to believe that Okem was dead. Had that been the case, I would have felt it in my soul. Our hearts were still intertwined.

* * *

One month to the wedding, Albert invited me to dinner. It was in June, the weekend after the Children's Day celebration. He agreed to pick me up early so we could avoid driving home in the dark. The boundary clashes had subsided, although there were still rumors of robbers and ne'er-do-wells in the streets. I took some time to apply my makeup, hoping to impress him as I hadn't seen him in days. He had visited the day before but missed me by a few minutes. Ifedi had seen him and accepted the dinner invitation on my behalf.

Albert took me to a lavish restaurant on the outskirts of Ide. He looked adorable in casual pants with a simple t-shirt and a jacket. I had on a fitted navy-blue dress, gold accessories, and red sandals. The wait staff were courteous, serving course after course of tasty dishes. For entrée, I had a pasta dish with an assortment of seafood and vegetables, and we also tried the popular *nkwobi* entrée.

While we ate, Albert regaled me with stories about the fires he had to put out as he slowly took on the affairs of the kingdom, and I shared the progress I had made with the wedding planning. A man and a woman walked hand-in-hand into the restaurant, and the man reminded me a little bit of Okem, especially as he kissed the lady on her forehead before he took his seat. They sat two tables away from us. Out of curiosity, I glanced in their direction at intervals, innocently pondering their status—if they were married, dating, or if they were just friends. I guessed I had glanced one too many times when Albert cleared his throat.

"Why do you keep looking at those two?" he asked with creased brows, his eyes piercing through mine.

"I don't know. It's just..." I said, shaking my head.

"Then focus," he said, slowly pointing his middle and index fingers back and forth at eye level.

"I'm sorry. That guy reminded me of Okem. I can't say what it is exactly, but when they first came in, I thought I'd seen a ghost."

Albert was quiet from then on. I realized something had gone terribly wrong when he grabbed my hand forcefully and walked into his room when we got to the palace.

"You embarrassed me today," he said, the moment he shut the door behind us.

"How?" I asked, stunned by his accusation.

"What was the point of that stupid display at the restaurant—behaving like a common tart? All because of that vagabond you insult my status," Albert berated me. "After everything I've done for you? After all this time since Okem left, not to mention our engagement that captivated the whole kingdom, you dare to bring up your servant boy as though I, Albert, am of no consequence."

"What the—"

The words were barely out of my mouth before his hand flung forward and landed on my left cheek. The cracking sound and the vibrations, starting from my temple and spreading all the way to my jaw, left me in a senseless daze. I stared at him wide-eyed as my hand slowly swept across my stinging face.

"Albert," I screamed, as a rage crept through my body.

"Shut up, or I'll do worse than slap you," he hissed as his entire body shook.

I froze to the spot, unable to cry as I tried to make sense of the attack. The only evidence that I was alive was the sound of my heart thumping in my chest, threatening to burst. I had never experienced such fury, not from him, my father, my grandfather, Okem, or any male I'd ever encountered. As he spoke, he pointed angrily at me. I remained still to avoid further assault. At the time I did not think to flee, I could not think anything. All I wanted was to understand the reason for the outburst. It had to have been for much more than the incident at the restaurant since the Albert I knew would never resort to using his strength to subdue a woman.

"Don't you have any shame? How can you, my fiancée, engage someone to look for a man, one that used to be your help? Don't you have respect?"

He spat his words as his eyes bored through mine. As I opened my mouth to respond, he threw a brown envelope, identical to the one Amah's uncle used to mail the results of his search for Okem at my feet. When Albert visited our home the day before, Ifedi, had accidentally handed him my mail when she gave him the RSVPs. A fatal error, only I didn't realize how fatal such an error could be until then. My head still reeling from the slaps I received, I picked up the envelope and slowly walked to the door.

"If it weren't for me, you'd be nothing," Albert continued. "His own family is so poor they discarded him for your grandfather to train. He may have lived under the same roof as you, eaten the same food as you, and learned some manners along the way, but he was always and will always be a nonentity. Your status as my bride to be has elevated you beyond what you can ever comprehend, and you dare sully that by mentioning that degenerate in my presence?

Don't you ever insult me like that again! Remember, you caused this. If you hadn't brought him up, none of this would have happened. Come let me drop you off!"

I walked behind him on the way to the garage. After we got into the car, he paused with his hand on the ignition and sighed. I could feel the heat coming from him, and I was sure he could hear my elevated heartbeat. We rode in silence until he pulled into my grandmother's gate.

"Goodnight," he said, in a voice so soft and calm, that no one could have guessed what he had just put me through.

I shut the door quietly without responding. As soon as I stepped into the house, hot tears ran down my face. *What just happened?* I asked myself repeatedly. The throbbing in my cheeks told me it was real. I held my face, which by then was devoid of any feeling as it had grown numb from the assault, and walked to my room. What I'd just experienced left me in despair. I felt like I was falling into a deep dark hole, my internal organs strangling one another as they struggled to make their way out of my mouth. I had never wished more than I did at that moment that my grandfather was still alive to protect me.

*　*　*

I cried myself to sleep that night. In the morning, I felt raw. I thought of Okem, and then my thoughts drifted to Albert. Since Albert had never assaulted me until then, I concluded the incident was a one-off resulting from my bad behavior. Searching for Okem behind his back was bad enough. Involving the entire world in that search was belittling.

Too ashamed about the incident, I swore not to breathe a word about it to anybody, especially not my grandmother. Telling her would mean revealing my role in the issue. I stuck to my convictions and told no one, not even Ifedi, who observed the marks on my face. I spent the rest of the day in my room to hide my distress. My grandmother left me alone. She must have thought I just needed to rest after my big date the night before.

Albert didn't let it pass. He came to see me in the evening. I met him in the parlor upstairs, away from the prying eyes of my grandmother.

"I am so sorry about yesterday," he pleaded. "Please forgive me. I don't know what came over me."

"It was the devil," I said, glaring at him.

"What?" he asked earnestly.

"The devil came over you."

He paused and knelt before me, and I looked away, disappointed he hadn't caught the slightest hint of my sarcasm.

"I swear," he said, touching the tip of his lip with his index finger and pointing it to the ceiling, "that I have never ever touched another woman in my life."

I turned to stare at his face in astonishment. I didn't know what I was searching for, but that last comment hurt me as deeply as his crime did. I must've been the worst kind of woman if someone as kind and as calm as Albert could raise his hand against me.

"What you did drove me insane," he continued, cutting through my reverie. "Please forgive me."

I remained still.

"I won't do it again," he pleaded. "Please, my darling. Please forgive me."

"I forgive you," I finally said when I couldn't bear his pleading any longer.

Although I believed the promise he made to never assault me again, the incident marred our relationship. One week later, after hours of pleading and uncountable gifts, I decided to really forgive him and blamed myself for provoking him.

CHAPTER TWELVE

IT HAPPENED AGAIN. Was this my punishment for choosing status and wealth over love? Was Albert my burden to bear for driving Okem away?

One night, after a protracted argument about something so insignificant I barely remember, Albert lifted me and threw me across my bedroom. As my head hit the wall, I became momentarily unconscious. Still dizzy when I came around, I froze until I saw him march out of the room and shut the door behind him. Realizing that what I thought was a one-off was actually a pattern of behavior, I cried until my eyes became sore.

I lay on the floor pondering how I got myself into such a situation. An hour later, I dragged myself to the sofa and sank further into sadness. Before I knew it, I was walking along the seashore in Luenah.

It was a particularly busy day. Familiar and unfamiliar faces roamed around, waving as they passed me by. For the first time, I noticed variations amongst the people. A number of the men and women, even the children, had a sad look about them. They looked down as they went by. Around their heads hung a wreath of dry weeds. The sorrow in their eyes caused me to briefly forget my own problems and ponder how a living being could be so bent out of shape. As I turned around the corner, my grandfather appeared and took my hand. We boarded the carriage *en route* to the shrine. On the way, he spoke softly to me.

"Remember the story of Jonah."

"Yes," I whispered.

"God sent Jonah to prophesy against Nineveh. But Jonah had other plans. He boarded a ship to Tarshish, and God sent a mighty tempest to threaten the sea and everything in it. Jonah's ship was at risk of destruction. His fellow mariners were afraid and did everything in their power to lighten the load in the vessel, hoping that would prevent them from drowning. When that didn't work, they prayed to their various gods to quell the tempest and cast lots to reveal the cause of their predicament. The lot fell on none other than Jonah, which forced them to throw him into the sea where a great fish was waiting to swallow him. Jonah remained in the belly of the fish for three days and three nights. He prayed and cried to God to rescue him and promised to do God's will if only He would honor his request. The third night, God spoke to the fish, and it vomited Jonah onto dry land."

My grandfather's voice was soothing. Like a balm, it eased the pain in my aching heart.

"Thanks for the refresher, Papa. I remember that story from my Bible study days as a kid."

"You're welcome, my dear. The challenge now is for you to understand how the lesson applies to you."

"You read my mind. What has Jonah got to do with me?" I said, shaking my head.

"How did you feel the first time Albert hit you?"

"Horrible. Albert has broken my heart to pieces."

"Why do you think he did it?"

"It was partly my fault. I…I hurt his feelings."

"Whose feelings are you responsible for, yours or his? Whose feelings matter more than anything else in this world?"

"I…I…don't—."

"Try, my dear. Whose feelings do you have control over?"

"Mine, I guess."

"Good! Tell me, after everything Albert has done to you, how do you feel about yourself?"

His questions perplexed me, but after a minute's pause, I responded. "Less than optimal. I can't even look at myself in the mirror. Grandfather, I'm *ashamed.*"

"I can see why, but you need never be ashamed of your struggle. It's the shame, not the struggle that will consume your self-worth."

I shook my head, trying to make sense of what he'd just said.

"But Papa, how could you have let him treat me that way? Couldn't you have helped me avoid this situation? Now, all I can think about is an escape but how can I? I've become so entangled in this mess."

"You had the power of choice and self-will. I couldn't save you from the situation. Not like you think. We all have to live with the consequences of our choices. As you know, the fact that you're an *Eri*, with access to Luenah doesn't exempt you from trouble."

"Am I being punished like Jonah?" I groaned. "Like Jonah, I should have known right from wrong. Papa, have I done an unforgivable thing by choosing Albert?"

"I don't think you fully understand, my dear. Jonah was not swallowed by the big fish as retribution for his crime. God doesn't derive pleasure in punishing His people. Jonah was swallowed to receive protection from the sea. Now, picture this. The belly of a whale is large. There was air. Jonah could breathe. Then, think of the alternative. If the whale had not swallowed Jonah, one of three things could have happened. He could have been swept away by a current, drowned, or been eaten by a shark. God allowed the whale to swallow Jonah, so He could protect him while He matured him. Even though he disobeyed God and stubbornly chose the path he thought would bring him happiness while ignoring directions, God still had a plan for him. Like Jonah, your entanglement with Albert does not signify the end of the road for you. Though it may sound ludicrous, you need to have faith and recognize that the situation may have arisen for your benefit. It may be God offering you protection and an opportunity to mature. What Albert did to you is an abomination, and it was not your fault, so you need to stop beating yourself up."

"I understand now, Papa, but I blew it. I'm sure all this has something to do with the box and the exchange it's supposed to receive. I felt it in my heart and soul the moment Okem disappeared. Even now, I still can't fathom what I should have given in exchange."

"Every choice we make has its own set of unique outcomes. You love Okem, but because you focused on pursuing what you thought would bring you happiness, you missed your chance to be with him. Even before Okem disappeared, you weren't sure if you should give up the comfort Albert could afford you for the plain life Okem would have given you. The fact that Okem eavesdropped on your conversation is irrelevant when you consider that the exchange was completed long before that fateful day. You weren't really sold on him, and he knew that in his soul. Exchanges have time limits. If one misses the chance to give the foremost exchange for love or duty and focuses on their quest for happiness, they must wade through life waiting and searching for the next opportunity to provide a worthy enough exchange to get them where they need to be."

"How long must I wait? And will things stay as they are?"

"I can't say, but here is an encouraging thought: We humans often miss the foremost path. Most times through our own fault and sometimes, through no fault of our own. No matter what, God will still deliver you to your destination. The subsequent paths will be more arduous than the foremost one, but regardless, you will learn all the lessons you need along the way. You may have missed your first route, but don't panic. Remain steadfast, and you will soon get back on the right track as soon as your exchange is complete."

"Encouraging? Yes. Calming? Not so much," I said through pursed lips.

He shrugged.

"If only you knew who walked with you, you wouldn't say that."

"But Okem is the only man I have ever loved. Is it too late? Will I ever see him again? Will I ever achieve my purpose? And what if someone doesn't give an exchange at all?"

"Of course, you'll still achieve your purpose," my grandfather said, shaking his head. "And if someone doesn't give an exchange at all, life will offer one for them. You see, my child, there are multiple paths to one's purpose, and exchanges are made at the point of choosing a path. If you fail to make the right exchange at any point in time, you may have difficulty getting on the right path, but you'll eventually get there. You're probably closer than you know. The detour does not have the power to keep you from your destination."

"I guess I missed my way then. I boarded a ship to Tarshish instead of Nineveh."

He chuckled. "You're only human, and you're still alive, so there is still a chance for you to turn things around."

"Haven't I already missed out on love? I'm sure Albert is not the one and Okem—"

"Shh," he said, placing his index finger over his mouth. "Be careful what you say. You should have learned the power in your words by now. Just like your thoughts, your words have immense power to either transform or sustain your reality. That is the power of invocation."

"I understand, Papa."

As he spoke, I sighted the pointed tips of the shrine in the distance. Something about the halo effect of the clouds around them, reminded me of the people I'd seen walking around earlier with wreaths over their heads. I opened my mouth to ask my grandfather about them, but he spoke before I could utter a word.

"You see," my grandfather continued, "I want to explain this without confusing you. The right love will impact your purpose, which, in return, will impact your duty. When all these elements work together in harmony, you find fulfillment—the greatest source of happiness. Like I've told you repeatedly, chasing happiness in isolation will get you nowhere. You can see where it led you with Albert."

"Love sounds so simple, yet it's the most complex thing I've ever encountered."

He nodded in agreement.

"Two things must occur for love to be manifested. The first is to believe you're worthy of love. The second is to love yourself—"

"But..." I said, cutting in mid-sentence.

He raised his index finger to stop me.

"I want to be clear about something. Love must not only be romantic. Agape, storge, and philia provide as much satisfaction as romantic love. Love, also, must not only be directed at humans. There can be passion—love for something, a hobby, or a skill. Whatever it is, find that person or thing you're in love with, or you're passionate about, and get on the path to achieving your purpose."

"How will I know what it is?"

"It will speak to you and appeal to who you are. It's that person or thing that congregates your likes, strengths, and talents. That person or thing that puts your heart at peace and gives it rest—your source of energy, freedom, and joy. Many choose the thing they believe will make them rich and happy and ignore their God-given path. This happens when they try to imitate others. Such people will forever be unsatisfied—constantly searching for true fulfillment. Like Jonah, they will have to go back and forth, even if it means being delivered back to their starting point until they get on the right path."

"Am I limited to one person or one thing?" I asked perplexed.

"No! Not at all," he said, shaking his head.

"You may have as many purposes as you have passions. Different phases of your life will demand different things from you. The key is to pay attention to the transitions as the exchanges are made on the edge."

"I've heard everything you've said, Papa," I said, sighing in relief. "I'll now have to figure out how to put it to good use."

"Believe in yourself. Acknowledge that all you've done to come to this point is enough. Some people are lucky and their purpose finds them. Others are not so lucky. You still have time to make up for your mistakes, but don't expect an easy ride. Gear up for the time ahead and don't forget: Nothing is ever as it seems."

* * *

I woke up more confused than ever. I felt in my bones that the last thing my grandfather had been trying to tell me was of great importance, but there was nothing I could do about it. I played his final words, "Nothing is ever as it seems," over and over in my mind, and got nowhere trying to figure out what he meant by that statement.

* * *

I desperately sought an escape from Albert from then on. My grandfather had said I needed to figure things out by myself, so I kept looking for ways to resolve the issue. I did not only have my family to contend with but also the entire town because of my position. The situation proved too difficult for me. I wished my grandfather had given me the answers directly in Luenah.

With the little I learned, I pretended to continue preparations for the wedding while I discreetly made attempts to arrange a position in a law firm I once interned in Ajidi. I feared Albert would resume using me as his punching bag if he sensed my disinterest. My grandfather's friend warned that breaking my engagement to the Crown Prince would be an act of treason. The crime bore serious consequences as I would be breaking an oath I made to the crown. He insisted that carrying on with my plan would threaten not only my existence but also that of my grandmother, my parents, Ifedi, and even Okem. It would be safer, according to him, for me and everyone in my household if I married Albert, as our lives could depend on it. His warnings, though terrifying, didn't change my mind about leaving Albert. I just needed to exercise caution. My grandmother was still in the dark about my tragic experience, and I intended to keep it that way until I had a sound solution for getting everyone out of the mess I had created. Everything my grandfather had been trying to tell me up to this point became so clear to me. I now considered my life as being separated into two sections; life before Okem and life after Okem. Before Okem, was carefree, fun, and glorious. After Okem, was constrained, dreary, and violent.

CHAPTER THIRTEEN

MY TURMOIL MULTIPLED when I received news
that Albert's father was sick. I feared that if he passed,
my fate would no doubt be sealed; I would be forced
to marry Albert in a hush-hush ceremony, and my
escape plan would be thwarted. It soon turned out
my fears were unwarranted. The moment news of the
King's illness hit the airwaves, the priority shifted
from the wedding to ensuring Albert was groomed
and primed to take the reins of power. The turn of
events gave a whole new meaning to the phrase *every
cloud has a silver lining*. It bought me much needed
time to put together a fool-proof plan.

The process began with three full days of rituals.
The first day, Albert, the kingmakers, and all the
titled men in Ide strolled along a dirt road that ran
across Ide and Ntebe. Accompanying them were men

in Albert's age group, several traditional dance troupes, and all the children who could sneak away from their homes to witness the historical event. The procession ended at the *Iba* shrine, a triptych mud structure, where ten cows were slaughtered at the entrance and presented as a sacrifice to the gods. Following this elaborate ritual, the massive crowd dispersed before sundown to prepare for the following day's festivities.

The next day, a procession gathered at the village square to witness Albert offer at least a hundred goats, fifty cows, and a thousand chickens as a sacrifice to the gods. Various age groups presented dances to the crowd and shouted adoration to the Crown Prince. As I watched the entire ceremony on the television from the comfort of our living room, I could sense the excitement in the air. But one person, I, was left out of it all. How could I be excited when my worst nightmare—getting married to Albert—was about to come true?

"You don't know how proud this makes me," my grandmother, who was sitting right beside me on the sofa, said, beaming with pride.

"I'm aware," I responded, trying hard to mirror her joy when inside, agony tore through me.

For weeks now, she had been preparing in earnest for me to take on my new role, completely oblivious of my state. I desperately wanted to tell her what I was going through but chickened out each time after convincing myself she would be too helpless to save me from the situation. No one could save me now, as I was in too deep.

I believed Ifedi had suspected something was wrong. I could tell because of the way she looked at me after I lied about a bruise on my arm. I had told her it came from hitting my hand carelessly against a wall when in fact it had come from Albert grabbing me too hard. Like my grandmother, I didn't see the point in telling her the truth, as she too would be incapable of rescuing me. I prayed for Okem to return. Being strong-willed, I was sure he would know how to get me out of the mess I was in. Amah's uncle had stopped searching altogether. After I called him a few times, and he didn't pick up my calls, I gave up. Albert had likely warned him against maintaining contact with me.

* * *

On Friday, after Albert had gotten over three days of hurdles, he marched to the palace with his entourage to complete the final task—to receive the staff of office—before the kingmakers crown him. A large procession waited outside the palace grounds. As Albert and the kingmakers were about to enter the hallway leading to the King's private chamber, two of the guards pulled Albert to a corner. They informed him that as the procession was heading to the palace, the King's attendants had found him lying motionless on his back when they entered his chamber to prepare him for the ceremony. They had tried to wake him up, and when all efforts failed, they had called the palace doctor, who confirmed he had been dead for hours. The palace insiders were immediately sworn to secrecy to avoid the mayhem that could occur from the news leaking prematurely.

In Ide, when a king dies, rites to appease the soul of the dead king and the ancestors consisted of burying the king with human heads to serve him in the afterworld. Head hunters are immediately put to task to obtain the required amount of heads to accompany the king to his grave before the masses catch wind of such a situation. For the quest to be successful, the oath of secrecy must be maintained. Any leakage and the masses would disappear from the streets for weeks on end until the burial is concluded and the kingdom declared safe from hunters, making it hard for the head hunters to achieve their goal. From the stories I was told since I was a little girl, the number of heads needed was a function of the king's age, his clout, and the number of years he'd sat on the throne. More heads led to a more successful reign in the afterworld, and in return, led to better intercession with the gods for the citizens that remained on earth.

While the procession waited outside, the palace began a propaganda onslaught, releasing lie after lie to cover for the real reason behind the cancellation of the crowning ceremony. The palace's communication secretary placed an announcement on radio and television stations to reassure the citizens that the King was in great shape and that the occasion would resume the following week. He even went as far as claiming that the King halted the ceremonies to prepare for the unexpected arrival of the powerful King of Farabar, who had insisted on witnessing the crowning ceremony. Many chose to believe the lies, but the discerning understood that something was amiss. By sunset, speculations about the fate of the ailing King increased. Whispers filled the air. The farms and markets slowly became deserted as many retreated inside from fear of what was to come. The next day, after an inside source leaked the news, the entire town was in shock.

* * *

With the King dead, our marriage was further delayed by ongoing traditional rites and customs, including acquiring the heads to accompany the King in his grave. Following a formal announcement that the King had died, the palace initiated a mourning period of one week and banned every form of celebration. Anyone found partying or merry making was arrested and made to serve penance, involving washing in the sacred river, a necessary cleansing rite for defiling the holy period. Since the reigning King died before handing over the staff, the King-in-waiting would have to go through the kingmakers, a process that took three weeks or longer and could result in unending chaos if another laid claim to the throne. To avert disaster, the first required course of action was a cleansing ritual for both the future King and the deceased King, making the process more arduous than if the staff was handed over without incident.

A wave of relief washed over me as the further away the wedding day moved, the more hopeful I became that my predicament might change. I'd been praying for a miracle, and it felt like my prayers had been answered. Albert's behavior was firmly beyond one slap too many. With each passing day my mind despaired over him. His nearness, his words, and even his touch when he hugged me, revolted me. Fear had clouded my existence in the past few months. Amah was lucky. She was going off to London to get her Master's. I now wished I had followed a different path.

"Don't worry," Amah had said when I visited her at her home in Ntebe. "I believe the cleansing will take care of things. You know something, Ona? I wonder if time isn't ripe to get rid of these archaic traditions—"

"What traditions?"

"Have you even been paying attention?" she asked, frowning. "Ona, where was your mind? I'm sure it was with your amazing fiancé."

I had only caught snippets of Amah's remarks. My mind had flown in different directions as we stood on her balcony enjoying the early morning breeze, watching as the orange glow of the rising sun appeared behind the trees. I glanced at her pretty face, admiring the bronze hue created by the sun's reflection on her left cheek, and shook my head.

"Did I say something wrong?"

"No. No. You didn't. I love that lipstick on you. It's very pretty."

I hadn't lied. Her lipstick was lovely, but more importantly, I needed so desperately to change the subject from Albert and me.

"Thank you!" Amah said excitedly. "I had no idea it was still there," she said, rubbing her lips. "I thought I washed it all off last night. You're very pretty too, my darling Ona. I know I marvel about Albert all the time, but believe me, he's the lucky one. *Ehen*, there's something I've been meaning to ask you."

"Go on. I'm all ears."

"Well, I've been talking to one of my friends from elementary school. Her brother just started a modeling agency in the UK, a big one for that matter, and they offered me to sign up with them. Do you think I should do it?"

"If you can find time during your studies, I don't see the harm in that. You have the looks, so why not?" She was crinkling her nose as I spoke. "What's the issue?"

"What will people think, though?"

"I'm not sure I understand, Amah. Which people are you talking about?"

"I have so many other things I'd like to pursue, but I always worry that people will make fun of me or judge me if I don't meet their expectations."

I laughed, in part, to relieve the tension in my head.

"That should be the least of your worries. People's opinions should never come between you and your dreams. That's as long as you're not trampling on anyone on your journey."

"You think so?"

"Listen, don't you know the fear of judgment comes from the need to be perfect?"

"Who wouldn't want to be perfect? *Eh?*"

"The way I see it, perfection should come from mastery, as mastery should come from doing. If I were you, I'd shift my focus to how I can uniquely improve myself every step of the way rather than worrying about what others think."

"That's right, Ona. How do you come up with this kind of stuff?"

"I don't know. It just comes to me," I said, grinning.

After several years going in and out of Luenah, I had acquired a lot of wisdom of my own. Unfortunately, none of the knowledge I was able to share now and then had enabled me to achieve what I needed the most. It certainly hadn't helped me with the perfect plan for a much-needed escape. Fear of repercussion had also deterred me from seeking help from the people that loved me. I had just returned from my bi-monthly visit to my parents, and despite the strong urge to tell my mother about my predicament, I resisted, knowing there wasn't much she could do in the present circumstance. Her constant affirmation that I had made something of myself didn't help either. I didn't think I would have her sympathy considering how independent I had become in everyone's eyes. I believed my position had somehow robbed me of my right to compassion. From the airport, I had gone straight to Amah's house, where I spent the night. The tension at home had become too great for me to bear. It was almost as great as the secret I carried in my heart. Somehow, it felt worse to keep it from my mother, grandmother, and Ifedi than from Amah. Amah thought I was the luckiest girl in the world. Being betrothed to the Crown Prince was every girl's wish—in her mind, at least. If only wishes were horses, I would gladly have traded places with her. But my condition was such that I wouldn't have wished it on anyone, not even my greatest enemy.

* * *

Following the cleansing ritual, the kingmakers invited

Albert to enter the palace sanctuary to seize the staff while they remained in the adjoining room. The crowd outside danced and rejoiced to the sound of loud music as they anxiously waited for the gunshots that would signal the successful lifting of the staff by their new King. This was the most anticipated portion of the ceremony. As soon as the staff was successfully lifted, a new era would begin in the history of the Ntebe people. Many hoped this era would usher in peace and ease the austerity measures imposed by the federal government to cushion the dwindling economy. But something strange happened when Albert tried to perform his rites, something that hadn't been witnessed by any person in the history of Ide. The staff refused to budge from its resting place, a stone altar in the sanctuary. Albert left the narrow space to inform the kingmakers. He persuaded them to perform further cleansing, hoping that would appease the angry gods. After several attempts, the staff still refused to move from its position. For two weeks, Albert returned daily to the sanctuary to repeat the action, but the staff remained fused to the altar. By the third week, rumors began to swirl as to the cause of the immovable staff. Some said the King's spirit still roamed, unwilling to let go, due to some unfinished business. Others claimed the King had placed a curse on the throne to punish the citizens for their iniquities. Additional rites were performed to clear the obstacles from the way, yet nothing seemed to work. Albert was still unable to pick up the staff after thirty days. The kingmakers argued that after a befitting burial for the late King, he would feel assuaged and be more willing to let go.

* * *

With the three month deadline required by tradition to bury the King fast approaching, and Albert still unable to take the staff, the focus shifted to giving the *Ideme* the most befitting burial possible. The entire kingdom became frantic as they were reminded of the imminent danger. Farming seized, and farmers resorted to sowing crops around their homes and managed whatever they could reap until the risk of getting captured by headhunters no longer existed. Market places also became deserted, and hunger reigned as people preferred to starve than have their heads accompany the dead King to the afterworld. Since the headhunters were known to first seek the required number of heads from feuding neighbors before plundering their own people, neighboring towns like Ntebe were forced to maintain vigilance during coronations. Travelers also kept their noses to the ground to avoid getting caught in the crossfire. These henchmen applied all kinds of techniques to catch their prey, from using saboteurs within families to instigating clashes and gathering the spoils until they got enough heads.

Since failing to bury the King the right way

carried its own set of consequences. Everyone offered unsolicited advice from the safety of their homes to ensure no stone was left unturned. Everyone, except me. If Albert couldn't pick up the staff, he could not be crowned the King of Ide, and I could not become his wife. To my relief, the wedding was postponed indefinitely, and I could not help but feel that everything was working altogether for my good.

CHAPTER FOURTEEN

AS PREPARATIONS FOR the *Ideme's* funeral began, bizarre incidents started occurring in Ide. Strange ailments struck both the young and the old, citizens disappeared in record numbers, and the soil became barren. Crops that were ready for harvesting suddenly withered and died. Fear gripped the populace. Rumors swelled that the gods were angry about the state of the town. Their wrath was so great that they needed more than the required human sacrifices to be appeased. There were claims that the *Ideme's* hunters and henchmen prowled the residential neighborhoods after midnight in search of victims. The whole town became infected with terror. Everyone retreated inside by dusk and remained so until sunrise. The tension in Ide transferred to Ntebe and my home.

"Ona, you have to avoid going out from now on," my grandmother pleaded when we sat down for dinner. "I know you're a grown woman now, but I have never seen such chaos in my life. I was a young girl when the last king was crowned, and though there was human sacrifice, it was not of this magnitude. I don't want to endure any more loss. Have you heard me?"

"Grandma, is this not mostly Ide's *wahala*? Is it not their problem? I know it's possible for the headhunters to prey Ntebe, but I always come back before dark. Besides, the only place I ever visit these days is Amah's house. Are you saying I shouldn't even go there?"

"Hmm, Ona. There is no difference between Ide and Ntebe when it comes to things like this. Our borders are so close that anything affecting one will trickle down to the other. Don't even visit Amah. If Amah wants to see you, she can come here. It's best to exercise caution in these times. Is it not better to be safe than sorry?"

"Grandma, I've heard," I said, reaching for her hand. "I don't want to be used to appease the gods of Ide. That will not be my portion."

My grandmother retrieved her hand and snapped both fingers, pursing her lips. "Yes, that will not be your portion," she reiterated. "You won't believe what I heard from the market women."

"What could be worse than what we already

know?"

"They need twenty heads."

"What?" I screamed as unease slithered down my back.

She nodded and began at once to fill her glass with wine.

"Two for every decade he has ruled and the rest for whatever reason I don't know. People are saying all kinds of things. I strongly believe all this has something to do with Albert not being able to take that staff."

"I can't believe these things are still happening in this day and age. Grandma, is this honestly real?" I asked wide-eyed.

"Yes, and by the look of things, they're bent on reaching their target. Do you know how many people were reported missing this past week? People are disappearing in record numbers. Hoodlums are also taking over. The timing has never been more perfect for people that feel they have a score to settle with their fellow human beings to attack. Murderers and ne'er-do-wells are seizing this opportunity to rob and kill and perform all manners of ills."

"But they'll get caught."

"No! They won't. Not if things get out of hand. They plan to get cover under the lawlessness that will surely follow."

I didn't know what to believe, but I took my grandmother's advice and stayed within the confines of Ntebe. Soon, the disorderliness resulted in the resurfacing of old ills. Rumors of pending clashes between Ide and Ntebe reached our ears. A curfew was set in Ntebe to avoid the actions of miscreants. The two towns were yet to recover from the last clash, which left several injured and many properties destroyed. Land that was previously ruled on by the courts, again, became a source for dispute. Cases that were assumed to have been settled several years back were reopened. Some of them were at least a hundred years old. The files had rotted, and the original owners of the land had long since decomposed in their graves. While all this was going on, security was fortified in Ntebe and businesses were closed to avoid pending destruction.

* * *

"I don't understand why you never leave Ntebe," Albert whined during an unexpected visit. "You never come around to see how you can help your man. Don't you see that I'm going through so much?"

With everything he had been going through, he had become a mere shadow of his former self. He barely even looked me in the eye as he spoke. It was as though he was trying desperately to hide something behind that crooked heart of his. I knew what it was. It was his shame. If only he knew how much I hated him. I was sure he had brought his problems onto himself, yet, I still felt sorry for him.

"Don't you see what I'm going through?" he repeated. He had become jittery when I didn't respond fast enough.

"I do see what you're going through, but I'm not sure how I can change the situation or make things better."

"You can take my side. That is your rightful position. That is what you've been trained to do all these months. Can you come over tomorrow?"

My grandmother shook her head fervently after Albert uttered those last words. Albert's back was facing her, so he hadn't noticed her reaction. My grandmother had seemed so engrossed in the program she was watching on the television that I was surprised she had overheard our conversation. In light of the current circumstances, her gesture, a demand for me to reject Albert's request, didn't surprise me. She always seemed to take his side in the past, but things were different now.

"I c—can't," I finally mustered the courage to say.

"Hmm! Why not? I need you now!" He said with pleading eyes.

"Is it safe for me to be running around Ide at a time like this?"

"What do you mean by is it safe? Nothing will happen to you. I can pick you up and bring you back before the curfew."

"What about the rumors?"

"What rumors?"

"The headhunters."

"That's nonsense."

He became angry, violent almost. Judging by the scowl on his face, I feared he may have forgotten for a moment that my grandmother was sitting right behind him. As though he'd read my mind, he calmed down immediately.

"As the future Queen, no one can touch you. You're guarded round the clock. I've also had your security tightened. But, I understand why you don't feel like moving around at this time. No worries. I'll be doing the visiting until things calm down, okay?"

"Okay, thank you." I was hoping things wouldn't calm down for a while. The old normal didn't work for me. I was craving a new normal—one that didn't include Albert.

After he left, I sat in a corner and glued my eyes to the television, but I could feel my grandmother watching me from the corner of her eye.

"Is everything alright?" she asked.

"Yes," I lied.

"Don't worry. Albert should understand that it's not safe out there right now. You can resume your marriage plans after he's overcome the insurmountable hurdles he's facing."

I was tempted to tell her the whole truth right there and then. Of recent, I had begun to fear for my life and wondered if I was doing the right thing keeping her in the dark. The coronation, the boundary clashes, and my role as Albert's future wife made me extremely anxious. I opened my mouth to speak, but something stopped me. It would put her life in danger if I confided in her. The thought of how she might react scared me. She may try something drastic and end up endangering our lives. The fact that my security had been tightened did not help matters. Though it was meant for my protection, it stifled the progress of my mission. Once Albert is crowned, I was expected to marry him in a quick ceremony. An escape was even more dangerous now. I started to doubt the possibility of one and even began to consider resigning to my fate.

CHAPTER FIFTEEN

I **KNEW SOMETHING** more dangerous was looming when the peaceful demonstrations began. My instincts were correct because in no time history repeated itself.

A full-blown clash occurred within one week of Albert's visit. Ide's youth gathered with guns and machetes, and a war for land ensued with Ntebe. Their King was dead, and the Crown Prince was having difficulty occupying the throne. This created room for anarchy, and since no one had enough authority to call them to caution, the different factions sought to show bravado and courage to lay claim to as much land as possible. It was merely a fight for power to defeat one's opponent through intimidation. Saboteurs arose within Ide. They sought to possess masses of land that were previously allocated to

Ntebe. Their plan was to dominate the region and claim the throne for their kinsman. The resulting battle was more turbulent than any that had ever been recorded in the history of the two towns. Armed policemen and soldiers were sent from the federal headquarters to calm the clashes. The warring factions shot at the policemen with sophisticated weapons and the federal troops fought back with extreme force.

After the fighting had gone on for days, the elders from both Ide and Ntebe decided to meet, albeit late. Thirty people had died, and hundreds were injured. Many businesses had been destroyed. Surviving ones remained closed for weeks as people hid indoors until they were sure calm had returned to the streets. The elders agreed to seek help outside of the leadership of the two towns to gain objectivity in resolving the boundary issues.

Within a few weeks, the regional government set up an administrative panel to review the cause of the recent clash. The panel spent weeks going over contracts, details, maps, and invoices to determine the root causes so they could resolve them once and for all. Following an exhaustive inquiry, they arrived at a consensus about the issue. The towns agreed to get things in order and maintain peace. To ensure the cases received fair judgment, they were all referred to the high court in Ajidi. A few of them, the most complicated ones, were considered best served if they were handled outside the country. Within weeks, court dates were set, and relative peace returned.

* * *

Albert was absent from the meetings that resulted in a final agreement to maintain peace between the towns. Though the peacekeeping committee had invited him to participate, he sent a representative to fill his spot, claiming that he had significant issues to resolve. The populace was losing faith in him. They blamed the clashes and the difficulties that befell Ide, including hunger and famine and all manners of ills, on his inability to occupy the throne. Pressure mounted on the kingmakers to find an immediate replacement. The kingmakers had started to doubt Albert's eligibility for the position. They had one final step to carry out before they threw the position open to the next in line—to consult the oracle, a powerful and unseen force for providing prophecies or punishment directly to recipients. The intermediary, the chief priestess, attempts to commune with the ancestors to understand their feelings about the condition of the land. One of two things could happen after a future king visits the oracle: they either return with the power needed to take on their new role, or they prepare to die within days of the divination. Should the oracle decree in favor of Albert, he would come out of the experience alive and get crowned King; otherwise, he may suffer dire consequences and pay with his life. No living being in Ide had ever witnessed such a calamity; the recently deceased King had ruled for fifty years, and the King before him had ruled for seventy, and both had assumed office without incident.

"Are you sure you need to go through this?" I asked Albert when I visited the palace in Ide. I no longer had an atom of feeling for him, but from what I'd heard about the oracle, it was not something to meddle with. It was an extremely dangerous venture, dangerous enough to prompt me to defy the odds and visit him. I needed to warn him.

"What other choice is there?" he asked, searching my face in anticipation.

"I don't know. There has to be some other way."

"I have tried everything in my power. There's no other way, my dear. I have to possess the staff. That's the only way there is."

I felt a tinge of sadness when I heard him say, "My dear." It reminded me of what we once were. If someone had told me that I could love someone one day and hate them the next, I wouldn't have believed it. Yet, here I was sitting across from Albert in his study and wondering what I really felt for him. Not hate, and certainly not love. I snapped myself out of my reverie as I remembered I had come there for a reason.

"This oracle business seems to be taking things to a dangerous level," I said. "I don't think you need to do everything the kingmakers ask you to do. Amah told me something the other day that resonated with me. She said it might be time to do away with these old traditions, and I agree with her. They're just too destructive at times."

"You both are right," he said, jumping out of his chair. "Why do I need this bunch of losers that call themselves kingmakers to take the staff? The throne is my birthright. The throne belongs to me. When I become king, I will banish those customs. I'll banish those men—"

I opened my mouth to speak, but he raised his hand to stop me.

"And I don't want to disappoint you," he continued, pointing at me. "You've already been groomed to be Queen. What will people think if we leave things as they are? *Eh*? And what about me?"

I cringed when he said 'queen', but he was too engrossed in his speech to notice my disgust. I glared at him as he continued to rant about what, and who he thought had caused his misfortune. He blamed his father, his mother, and even blamed me. He claimed my waywardness had somehow come in the way. Halfway through his rant, he announced, "I'm sure you know what I'm talking about."

"I don't know," I said, easing back into my chair and regretting ever coming to visit him.

The longer I looked at him, the more I realized my folly. *How could I have chosen this one over Okem?*

Oh no, I didn't actually choose him, I quickly reminded myself. He appeared out of nowhere.

His features had grown pale, and his beard was scraggly. Things seemed to be getting worse for him.

"Forgive me," he said, jolting me from my reverie.

"For what?"

He sighed deeply and walked towards me to take my hand.

"I'm just lashing out at everyone," he said in a pleading tone. "Promise me you'll never, ever, leave my side. Please. You're the only one I can count on. Everyone seems to have deserted me."

I felt sorry for him. There was no use in kicking someone who was already down, so I simply nodded. He must have sensed my hesitation.

"You won't ever leave me. Will you?"

I shook my head, afraid that his miserable mood may soon turn to anger, and his anger to my getting punched in the face.

"No. I won't."

* * *

That night, I dreamt that something was chasing me, and I woke up suddenly, drenched in sweat, as a powerful feeling overcame me. My heart was pounding, and I felt paralyzed with fear. Feeling extremely clammy, I got up to change into a different nightgown. My heart was now beating steadily, and I was afraid but couldn't figure out why. I remembered that Amah was leaving in a few days, so I picked up the phone to call her but stopped as I realized it was only 3 AM. Throwing my head against my pillow, I stared at the ceiling and pondered my next move. Thirty minutes later, I walked downstairs to the kitchen for a drink. I jumped in fright when I turned on the lights and saw Ifedi sitting on a stool, a stone-cold look registered on her face. It took a moment for her to realize I was standing there.

"Ona, you're up?" she scolded when she finally came to her senses.

"Ifedi, what are you doing in the dark? Is something wrong?"

"I couldn't sleep."

"I couldn't sleep either. Maybe it's the heat. Sorry to intrude, but I needed some water."

She didn't respond, so I got what I needed and left, while she remained seated in her position. When I got to my room, I placed the now empty cup on the side table and cranked up the air-conditioning before sliding under the sheets. Still having difficulty sleeping, I stayed up till sunrise, and the moment the clock struck 5:59, I called Amah.

"What time is it?" she asked. "What happened? Has Albert lifted the staff?"

"I don't know about Albert lifting any staff. I wanted to wish you a safe trip."

"But it's not even six, yet. Couldn't you have

waited until the morning? Not that I mind, but I thought something important happened."

"Sorry Amah for getting you so excited. It's just that I've been staring at the ceiling for hours after a terrible nightmare woke me up."

I described my dream to Amah, right to the last detail.

"What do you think that was about?" she asked.

"I don't know. I visited Albert earlier in the day, and we talked about the oracle. That must have entered my subconscious and manifested in my dream."

"That's likely what happened. Why do you think Albert hasn't been able to take the staff? Ona, you have to pray *oo*. This is no joking matter."

"Do you think I don't know that? The thing is giving me a serious headache. Soon you'll leave me to deal with all these problems on my own. I'll miss you so much."

"I'll miss you too. It's a pity that I won't be able to attend the wedding when it finally happens."

I burst into laughter.

"What's funny?"

"Nothing. It's just that you're looking forward to the wedding more than I am."

"Yes *o*," she said with a chuckle.

I still hadn't told her about my issues with Albert. Now that she was leaving, it would simply be torture letting her in on it, and I didn't quite think she'd understand. Albert was usually sweet. It would have taken great effort to convince anyone he was capable of lifting his hands against a woman.

"Don't forget to send your address the moment you get to London, and take good care of yourself."

"I will, my dear Ona. I'll write to you as soon as I settle down."

"I trust that you will, and I'll be praying that everything works out right for you."

"Thanks, love. You, too."

* * *

After I hung up the phone, I lay down to try and get some sleep. As I was reminiscing about Amah, Albert, Okem, and everyone that had impacted my life so far, I felt a familiar sensation and slowly drifted to Luenah. My grandfather took me to the shrine and showed me the image of a man on a screen.

"Do you remember this face?" he asked.

"I recognize him," I said. "That was Ozumba— Okem's father. I remember that many years ago, he had brought Okem to live with us. Back when Okem was just a scrawny little dancing boy."

"You were little yourself too, although I wouldn't call you scrawny."

I laughed and continued to stare at the image. It was definitely Ozumba. He looked a lot older than I remembered, and he had the wreath of weeds on top of his head, the same as I'd seen some people wearing the last time I was in Luenah. He was shriveled as an old fruit, as an unripe mango plucked before it was ready to be eaten and left in the sun.

"What is that?" I asked.

"A mark of dishonor," my grandfather whispered.

"Is that why he looks so miserable? Why does he bear the mark? Why is he in Luenah? Is he an *Eri* too?"

"He is."

"Then why was he dishonored?" I asked in a desperate tone.

"One thing you must know is that Luenah, even with all its strengths, has its weaknesses, too. The decisions by some *Eri*, disrupt the balance in this mystical world. Some of the members choose to be evil despite the good nature that's bestowed on them. These same people find ways to use their spiritual powers to penetrate the minds of others to garner support for their quest to topple the seat of power so they can do as they please, mostly bad. Though peace and tranquility are some of the things we enjoy in Luenah that make it superior to other realms, there have been massive obstructions to this peace by the actions of these few. Luenah has zero-tolerance for evil, so to combat this problem, the supreme ruler created the spell of detection a hundred years ago after a massive rebellion threatened the throne and resulted in various syndicates vying for possession of our realm."

"There was a rebellion?" I asked, stunned. "I simply can't imagine it. How does the spell work?"

"The wreaths."

"What about them?"

"The one you saw on those people's heads, including Ozumba's. Those mark them as the bad eggs. Anyone can detect them from miles away."

"What if they continue to rebel? The wreaths alone can't stop them."

"You're right. It can't. It's meant for others to detect them, but they've been stopped for good. An illusion has been cast over their minds' eyes, so much that they can't see what you and I see. These lush fields, beautiful rivers, the peace, not to mention the shrine, are invisible to this bunch. In their place, they see dry land, muddy waters, and indescribable strife. Luenah looks inhabitable to them. Remember the darkness you experienced recently?"

"Yes," I said agitatedly. "I was going to ask you for an explanation but you vanished before I got the chance."

"I'm sorry about that, my dear."

"That's okay, Papa. Why did light leave?"

"There was a recent attempt in Luenah. Since the olden days, when those attempts happen, our ruler imposes darkness until the offenders are identified, marked, and an illusion cast upon their mind."

"I didn't know *Eris* could do evil."

"*Eris* are human. Any *Eri* who has strayed so far they have little or no chance that they will accomplish their destiny is marked. With that sign over their heads, they lose all power to challenge the status quo."

"Hmm...I hope I never become like them."

"I don't think you have it in you, though humans can be unpredictable."

My mind went back to Ozumba.

"What about Ozumba? What did he do to put himself in this position?"

"That is between him and his *chi*."

"Why can't his *chi* help him out of the situation?"

"Remember, *Onye kwe chi ya ekwe*. If one agrees, her spirit will agree also."

"Oh...I do. But—"

"You ask too many questions, my dear. I can't tell you any more now, or it'll disrupt the balance, and that may not be in your favor."

"Tell me one thing, Papa."

He shook his head."

"Just one more thing," I pleaded.

"Is your question about Okem?"

"How did you know, Papa?" I asked with trepidation.

"It's written all over your face."

Ozumba was Okem's father. I feared that if

Ozumba was in trouble then Okem could be in trouble too.

"Is Okem all right?"

"Be patient. Everything will be revealed at the right time," he chided me.

"What about me? Has this got—?"

Before I could complete my question, I found myself drifting into consciousness and the real world again.

I cried for the first time after a visit to Luenah, having lost control of my emotions. My grandfather and Okem were the most important people in my life, and I missed them. I wondered what it would be like to have both of them by my side at that moment. I felt lonely and trapped and desperately out of my mind. My grandfather was right. Everything I thought I wanted as a kid and would have as a grown-up—love and happiness—had turned around and caused me so much misery and desperation. I had nowhere else to turn, and I was angry at my grandfather for not helping me through this trying time. Then again, I knew he was acting in my best interest. He had explained the way of Luenah several times. Everything had its ebb and flow. The things that needed to be revealed were gradually exposed to avoid tipping the balance.

CHAPTER SIXTEEN

THE SCENE WAS set as it had been every Sunday since my travails with Albert began: Grandmother was in the kitchen preparing a delicious meal in a large pot; Ifedi was whistling tunes under her breath as she set the dining table, orange streaks from the evening sun streamed through the cracks in the curtains, and I pretended to be reading the novel in front of me while in reality I was crying inside and praying fervently for my lot to change.

From the corner of my eye, I noticed Ifedi edging her head sideways to glimpse the cover of my book.

"You seem so engrossed," she said. "What's the book about?"

If only she knew how engrossed I was with the issues hampering my existence, I thought, *she wouldn't have dared interrupt me.* My last encounter with Papa still weighed on my mind. He had tried to show me something, Okem's father, Ozumba. I wondered if he was trying to show me Okem instead, to let me know where he was, where I could find him. But Ozumba had a mark on his head. What did that have to do with Okem?

"Ona! The book...you haven't answered me. What's it about?"

Ifedi's call shook me out of my reverie.

"Oh! It's…" I flipped it to read the blurb.

"You don't know what you're reading? How is that possible? You've gone past the middle."

She was right. I didn't know what the book was about. I hardly read past the title.

"Why can't you leave me alone, Ifedi?"

For some time now, Ifedi had been paying particular attention to me, pushing my buttons at times to get me to open up. If I didn't know better, I would say she was intentionally trying to annoy me. So much was going on around me that I couldn't control, but this minor issue was within my control.

"What's eating you up, Ona? *Na wa oo.*"

I glanced at her and shook my head. There was no point in responding. I knew the case was closed when she cast a bewildered look around, and my grandmother smiled mischievously. Silence fought and won with a landslide victory. The time was ripe to dispel all the negative thoughts in my head to maintain the sense of power I felt at that moment. As fate would have it, it turned out that I didn't have to try too hard. Something significant happened to change my lot.

* * *

Grandmother, Ifedi, I, and the myriad of guests we entertained that evening came and left, and I retired to my room. Exhausted, I tried reading my book, hoping it would help me fall asleep. Near midnight, there was a soft knock on the door. Before I had the chance to look, it opened slowly, and an image appeared in the shadows. Okem was standing there, with his index finger over his lips, urging me to remain calm.

"Shh…" he said when he saw the startled look on my face.

"Okem," I whispered, my heart pounding. "Is this really you? I can't believe my eyes right now! Where have you been?" I jumped out of bed and ran to him.

Two strides and his arms were around me, squeezing me.

"How have you been, my love?"

A gasp escaped my lips.

"You have come to rescue me," I said, breathing heavily.

"We will rescue each other," he whispered. "How are you? I'm sorry for startling you."

"I'm fine now! I'm so happy to see you."

He seemed taller, darker, and much more handsome than when he left. He was now distinguished-looking too, highly distinguished as a matter of fact. Wherever he'd been, I was certain he'd made a fortune for himself. I remained in his embrace, my heart beating uncontrollably, feeling as though I was going to collapse. But his arms, those strong arms, holding me close to his chest, kept me grounded. He smelled amazing, like flowers in full bloom. I started to sob quietly, and then I pinched myself to make sure I wasn't dreaming. No. *This was real.* Hot tears streamed down my face and spilled all over his expensive cotton shirt, but he continued to hold me firmly, his chest pumping furiously against mine. We held each other for what felt like an eternity before he broke our hug, looked into my eyes for a fleeting second, and then pressed his lips against mine. I had not expected such a sensation from a kiss. His tongue against mine created an electrical charge that ran through my spine, down to my toes.

I was still so lost in our world when he slowly released his lips from mine and muttered, "Why did you choose that brute?"

"Okem, why did you abandon me?" I asked, looking into his eyes.

"I had no reason to stay. I tried to prove to Ifedi that you were only using Albert and that I was the one you truly loved, but I heard you praise him and belittle me when Ifedi posed the question to you. You broke my heart, Ona. I thought it was best for me to disappear and let you have the life you thought you deserved. I couldn't stay and let everyone feel sorry for me."

"Yes, Ifedi told me you were listening at the door," I whispered.

"It was a shameful thing for me to do, but I'd hoped it would help resolve your indecision. I regret it all now seeing as it back-fired."

"It back-fired more than you know," I said, sighing.

"How do you mean?" he asked, moving my shoulders a few inches away to look at my face.

"Okem, if you had listened a little longer, you would have heard me choose you. What you didn't know was that I had actually chosen you over Albert. You ran off before you had the chance to hear me proclaim my undying love for you. A part of me died that night, and I was left to live with the remnants."

"I don't understand. What do you mean by you chose me?" he asked, kneeling before me and holding my hands.

I recounted what really happened the night he disappeared. After I was done, he sat on the edge of the bed, held his head with both hands, and sobbed.

"Ona, I didn't know," he said, choking on his words.

"You caused me so much pain. You should have

trusted me. You should have stayed to hear everything I had to say. See what your rash decision got both of us. For so long, I wondered if you truly loved me."

"Truly loved you? Didn't I ever tell you I would give my life for you? I left because I thought you had made your choice. I didn't see how I could compete for your affection with the *Ideme's* son. I didn't want to stay and cause shame and embarrassment for you either. And I certainly didn't think I could survive without you, so I chose what I thought was the lesser of the two evils."

"I was devastated when you didn't return. Having you leave like that, thinking I really thought those terrible things of you, destroyed my joy. Oh, Okem, how could you have been so gullible? You should have known how I really felt about you."

"I didn't know," Okem said with a sigh. "I wish I had trusted you."

He held me close as I sobbed quietly on his shoulder.

"I never planned to give you away. I always planned to come back after I had made it on my own, just like I promised you many years ago."

* * *

It hadn't even occurred to me to ask Okem how he made it to my room in the first place. The only illumination in the room had come from the full moon, dangling low and drenching one half of my bed with its soft lunar light.

"You'll get in trouble, and the guards might see you," I said.

"Which guards?" Okem asked with a sly smile.

"Didn't you see the men patrolling the grounds? I'm surprised they didn't stop you. They've been here since the chaos."

"Don't worry, darling. I took precautions to avoid that. I've been scoping this area for days. My driver parked a good distance away, at the bottom of the hill, and I got my men to draw their attention to something else while I snuck in through the side gate with the help of the gardener."

"Oh!" I said, chuckling. "Okem, you haven't changed one bit. You're still the same person on the inside."

"I had to stay the same for you."

We stared at each other for another long while. From my observation, judging by the physical, Okem had changed so much. He also exuded so much confidence, so much more than I had always known his self-assured self to have. It felt as though I was looking at a different person.

"Okem."

I was barely audible.

"My Ona," he responded and held my hands. "I love you so much."

"How much?"

"How much? I can't possibly explain. The extent is beyond what my commonsense would have allowed. Why? Because for all the pain you've caused me, I still felt that life would be one big hole without you. I have loved you my whole life. I even loved you the whole time I was away. When I learned of your engagement to that beast, I still loved you, but I couldn't save you."

I resisted the urge to cry.

"You knew? That he was abusing me?"

"I know everything that has gone on since I left. I was even at your engagement."

I gasped in astonishment.

"What?"

He nodded.

"I was. In disguise, anyway. It was the most painful thing I'd ever witnessed."

"I can't believe this. Each moment of the engagement ceremony, I was praying for you to creep out of the shadows and rescue me."

"I would if I could have. I would have given my life for you." His voice lowered to a whisper. "A lot is going on that you don't know about. I'll need you to come and see me tomorrow."

"Can't you stay a little longer?"

"I can't, at least, not now. Remember the guards. I have timed my exit to avoid an encounter. I'll tell you everything tomorrow; everything that has transpired since I left. Wait until tomorrow."

"Well, now I won't be able to sleep. Can you tell me the most important part now?"

"It's a long story. Come to the Palisir hotel around five." He was whispering again. "I'll explain everything then. Come alone, please. Not even with Amah. I'll be waiting for you in my room. I can't meet you at the lobby to avoid being seen together, but one of my men will be there to make sure no one bothers you. Come to room 765, and please do all you can to disguise yourself. I hope you understand what I mean."

He slowly released my hands and stood up to leave, his words lingering, leaving me in a panic.

"Don't hesitate, please. Our lives may depend on it."

"Our lives?"

He nodded, pursing his lips.

"You need to tell me what I'm up against," I shrieked.

He placed a finger on my lips before bending to kiss them.

"You will be fine. I'll explain everything tomorrow, okay?" he concluded before sneaking out the door.

The moment he left, all the questions I wanted to ask him tumbled around in my head: where he'd been all these years, how he had fared, and what gave him the courage to return considering the state of things in Ntebe and its environs? None of that mattered anymore. All that mattered now was that he was back and that he still loved me. I cried from joy and relief. I continued crying even when I saw Ifedi at the door.

"Everything okay?" she asked, a bewildered look on her face.

I nodded.

"Everything is okay."

"I just saw Okem leaving. What did he want? Where has he been?"

"I don't know. He was in such a hurry to leave, so we didn't get the chance to discuss at all."

"Why did you let him in after all this while?"

"I didn't. He just appeared—"

"He can't just appear. You must have known he was coming." She stuttered.

"What's your problem, Ifedi?" I said, hoping to calm her down.

She sighed and clapped her hands in derision. "My problem? How can you ask me that, Ona? Don't you know you shouldn't ever be alone with him? It could jeopardize your new status. You need to understand that things can't go back to the way they were. You're about to be married."

I was too excited about Okem's return to risk getting into an argument with Ifedi. Judging from his tone, it was important to maintain absolute discretion at this point, so I ignored her, hoping she'd walk away.

"Ona, answer me," Ifedi continued in a raised tone.

My heart skipped a beat. I feared that if I didn't offer a substantial apology, she might get hysterical and wake my grandmother up.

"I'm sorry, Ifedi," I said, pressing my hands together and flashing a wan smile. "I apologize for letting Okem in and creating the wrong impression."

"Please be careful from now on. Do you hear me? I'll see you at breakfast."

"I will. Have a good night. Please shut the door behind you."

"Good night," she muttered and crept behind the door.

I hardly heard her. My head was filled with Okem, my soul mate, my angel, my everything. I sat up on my bed and held my cheeks with both hands as the sounds of her footsteps faded in the hallway. An hour later, my heart still beat uncontrollably as I remembered Okem's strong arms, beautiful eyes, and the shock waves that swept through my body when he held me close to him. And the kiss? Phew! I said a prayer and did something my grandfather always cautioned me against—praying for sunrise to come. According to him, it was an inefficient prayer that robbed souls of a good night's sleep. In the meantime, there was nothing I could do. There was to be no sleep henceforth. My heart was filled with joy from seeing Okem. It was as though the past year had gone backwards to reset things to how it used to be between us. I wished I could call Amah so I could tell her that something had happened to my heart. I shuddered when I recalled I had to see Albert in the morning. He was traveling to Ghana in the afternoon. My meeting with Okem was scheduled for later in the afternoon. I needed to be careful. The tone of Okem's voice when he said, "our lives may depend on it," was not to be taken lightly.

CHAPTER SEVENTEEN

A FEW HOURS before I was scheduled to see Okem at the Palisir hotel, Albert sent his driver to pick me up from home. We had planned to catch an early lunch to discuss our wedding plans before he left for Ghana. Filled with dread at the thought of seeing him, not to mention the possibility of getting stuck at the palace, I opened the window to take in the fresh April breeze during the hour-long ride to Ide. It was the rainy season, but the first rain was yet to fall. Observing the sky, with the clouds of dust hovering beneath, and the leaves on the trees rising and falling like the flap of a wing, I closed my eyes and said a little prayer. I was tired of the dryness, so I asked for rain. At first, it was a slight drizzle; the faint scent of new rain met my nostrils. In the twinkling of an eye, it was falling in droves. I wasn't sure what the right sequence of events was. It was either I willed the rain to pour, or the rain was predestined to fall and by default motivated my senses to will it. Whichever it was, I shuddered at the fatalistic nature of the occurrence and settled down to enjoy the powerful earthy smell of new rain. We passed a picturesque square and a narrow two-lane street that stretched into a busy main road. On both sides were a jumble of buildings in no particular architectural style, just one in front of the other and another on top of the other, mix-matched and unsightly. Some were roofed with rusted aluminum sheets, others with cement. The larger ones had fences that were as high as the buildings themselves.

"Crazy city," I murmured to myself.

"*Nah so sistah,*" the driver responded.

I had forgotten I was not alone. He'd startled me for a second.

"*Nah the boundary clashes cause am o,*" the driver continued in broken English, craning his neck to look in the rear-view mirror.

"I know. These greedy politicians acquire large parcels of land that belong to the masses and build all these structures without proper planning and approval."

"*Nah true talk be dat.*"

I nodded, and he returned his attention to the road.

Slum city would be a better moniker for these

environs, I thought. Maybe Albert will address this if he becomes king. Albert. I completely forgot. The sights on the road had consumed me. I sighed as I thought of what I would say to Albert. Not at this meeting, only when the path was clear for me to pursue my relationship with Okem. I also dreamt of being far away, where Albert couldn't hurt me when I finally say those things to him. I would make sure he regretted ever meeting me, asking me to be his wife and daring to lay his dirty hands on me. I pictured the look on his face when that opportunity finally came, and I smiled. I could see it so clearly—the growl, the pain, the confusion, and the bitterness of a man whose only show of strength lay in terrorizing women who were weaker than him. As we rounded a bend that put us on the straight road that led to the palace, I tried to divert my mind to happier thoughts to avoid sinking into depression. At the gate, I forced a smile to appear on my face to avoid raising suspicion. The rain had stopped suddenly too, without warning.

* * *

I met Albert in his study. He seemed unusually distracted, but he managed to get up and kiss me on the cheek. Moving from place to place with a look of confusion in his eyes, he peered into shelves, searching for something.

"What are you looking for?" I asked.

"A contract. I kept it right here," he said, pointing at the desk."

"Have you checked those drawers?" I asked, pointing at the antique chest on the wall. "What does it look like? I can help you look for it."

"Oh, never mind. Here it is," he said, pulling a folder from his suitcase.

I heaved a sigh of relief and tried to relax on the settee. I struggled to keep my joy out of his view as we sat down to eat in the study after a uniformed servant brought us *fufu* and vegetable soup.

"Why aren't you eating?" Albert asked, staring at the morsel I placed on my plate.

"I'm eating," I protested. "I had a bit too much last night, so I'm still full."

I was full with Okem. How could I eat when Okem was back, waiting for me at the Palisir hotel?

"That's disappointing," Albert said, cutting through my reverie. "I asked the chef to make your favorite soup. He'll be disappointed you hardly touched any of it."

If Albert knew that I'd seen Okem the night before, I would be sorry. He hadn't laid his hand on me since his father died, but I knew he could reignite that monster. I had blamed myself the times he hit me. After each episode, he would remind me it was something I had done or something I had said that had triggered him. For a while, I struggled with my self-esteem, especially as he claimed he had never hit another woman besides me. Borrowing my grandmother's words, that was adding insult on top of an already painful injury. What was it about me that made him want to hit me? I asked myself often. What, about me, infuriated him so much, yet he claimed to love me so much, more than any woman he'd ever met? I no longer struggled with my sense of worth. I have long since figured out that it was never about me. It was always all about him. He was sick. More so, he was a coward and a loser. He would never have done what he did if he didn't think he could get away with it. That phase of my life was over. I knew there was only one way to go, and I felt sorry for the entire city and the tax money that was spent on my queenly training. I vowed to repay every penny when I could. But at that moment, I had other things to worry about. I had to hide all indications that I was seeing Okem that afternoon because if Albert knew, he would do everything in his power to make sure I never set my eyes on him again. I needed to protect Okem.

* * *

I left to see Okem after Albert's driver drove me home. Luckily, Albert wasn't due back for two days, so I didn't need to worry about stumbling into him. Okem was stunned when he saw me at his door. My disguise—a short wig and fake reading glasses—had worked magic. The moment he closed the door of his suite behind us, he held my waist and kissed me passionately with my back against the door. I was breathless by the time he released me.

"There seemed to be something urgent you wanted me to know," I muttered, reminding Okem why I was there.

"Oh! I'm sorry, Ona," he said, chuckling. "I've missed you so much. Seeing you again is like a dream come true."

"I can't believe it, either. Seeing you has erased the pain of these past months."

Together we entered his room, and he wasted no time filling me in on the details.

"Do you recall when I used to play the role of prince? When we were kids?"

"Of course, I do. I remember very well."

I remembered it like it was yesterday. That was when I was still allowed to play freely with Okem. He often played the role of a prince, a persona that took different forms over the years. Once, he pretended to be 'the frog prince' who had been charmed by a wicked witch. To break the spell, he stuck his lips out to kiss me, his 'beautiful princess' and I reminded him that if he didn't put his mouth right back where they belonged, his lips would remain protruding like that of a frog and he may indeed turn into one. He had shivered from fear over my comments and never played that game again. Another time, he was the knight, and I was his damsel in distress who he had come to rescue from the wicked witch who had the beautiful damsel holed up in a tower, banning her from seeing the man she loved.

"Those were the good old days," Okem said, jerking me out of my reverie. "Have a seat."

I sat on the desk while he sat on the bed, facing me.

"The father Albert has known his whole life, the late King is not his real father."

I shook my head in disbelief. "That doesn't make sense. Who then is his father?"

"His real father is Ekema's lover, Ozumba."

"Which Ekema? The King's sister? And Ozumba? How?"

"Yes, the *Ideme's* sister."

"But how?"

He sighed. "For years, Ekema nursed the ambition to control Ide and everything in it, including taking the throne. She saw her chance after her child was born two days apart from the King's real son. Her ambition drove her to perform a dastardly crime. At birth, the Crown Prince and her son Albert bore such a striking resemblance, like all children do, especially those born within the same family. When he was taken from his crib and replaced by her newborn son, no one, not even my beloved mother knew of the crime that was committed."

"Your mother!" I was on the edge of the desk, gasping for breath as I tried to make sense of the stunning revelations. Nothing Okem told me about Ekema and Ozumba, and now, his mother, made any sense. "What has your mother got to do with this?" I asked.

"My mother…the Queen."

"Wait! The Queen is your mother?"

He nodded once.

Stunned beyond belief, I placed a hand over my gaping mouth and the other on my chest to control the heaving. I had been struggling to absorb the fact that Albert was Ekema and Ozumba's son before Okem made the most shocking revelation of all.

"The Queen is my mother, and Ozumba, the father I have known my whole life, is not my real father. The late King is my father. It turns out that my role-play was not in vain after all. I am the Crown Prince."

* * *

I took a moment to take in everything Okem had just revealed to me and shivered as his comments hit me like a déjà vu. It reminded me of the out-of-body experience I had with the rain on my drive to Albert's house. It seems all these years, his role-play as prince, much like my wish for rain, was a type of prophecy.

"Go on," I pleaded after I realized he was waiting for his revelations to sink in.

"To ensure I was nowhere near the palace after she got her son settled into my rightful position,

Albert's real mother, Ekema, placed me with her boyfriend Ozumba and paid him handsomely to assume the role of my father."

"I can't believe this. Just to be sure, is this the same Ozumba I know?" I asked, feeling as though I would faint.

"Yes."

"How did Ekema explain the disappearance of her child?" I stood up from the desk to pace the room in every direction while Okem remained sitting on the bed with both hands on his knees.

"She claimed he died soon after birth. Everyone thought she'd lost her child."

I snapped my fingers in derision.

"Unbelievable. Thank God she didn't murder you."

"I heard she tried many times without success. Anyway, Ozumba took care of me for several years before he finally sent me off as a *house-boy* at Ekema's request. As I grew older, I began to look more and more like my birth father than my cousin Albert did. Ekema became increasingly scared that I would one day trace my lineage."

"I see that now," I whispered. "The resemblance is striking. You're the Crown Prince," I said, stopping for a few seconds to stare at him.

Okem remained calm and nodded slowly before continuing. "Some weeks before I was given away, Ozumba overheard me saying that I was a prince while I played with other children. He beat the living daylights out of me. It was soon after that declaration that they plotted to send me away; to make me disappear forever. An obscure servant would never see the light of day, so when your grandfather sent an emissary to Ide to look for a house-help, they found the perfect opportunity to get rid of me. Ozumba hatched a plan which Ekema readily agreed to. The emissary chose me after he was introduced to Ozumba, who at the time lived under the guise of a doting single father that needed all the help he could get in raising a child. Within a couple of days, I traveled to Ntebe with Ozumba and his cousin who posed as my mother."

"That was his cousin? The woman that came with you and Ozumba the day you moved in with us? I thought she was your mother?"

"They made me believe my mother had died during childbirth."

"Wonders shall never cease," I said, trembling from the shock.

"That was how I came to live with you. The arrangement was perfect, or so they thought. I was far away from Ide. What they didn't know was that your grandfather was not looking for any ordinary help. He wanted someone to double as a playmate for his little granddaughter. Your grandfather fell in love with me. That solidified the agreement."

"I know. Papa truly loved you."

Okem smiled and tears started to form in his eyes.

"Your grandfather never treated me like a servant. I think he saw something in me. We bonded the first time we met, and I really loved him too. Come here. You look as though you're going to collapse any moment. Come and sit beside me."

I shook my head. "I'm really confused. I can't sit still right now. None of this is coming together for me."

Okem stood from the bed and walked towards me. Stretching his hands, he pulled me close to stop the trembling. I held onto him and placed my head on his shoulder.

"Everything will be all right, Ona."

"I missed you, Okem," I finally said when I found my voice again. "I'm so happy you've come back to me."

"I missed you too, my love."

We held onto each other for a while before I released his back, slowly took his hands and looked into his eyes.

"I'm curious. How did you survive all this while? Where were you?"

"You won't believe all I went through if I told you."

"Tell me. I want to hear everything."

"It turns out nothing is hidden under the sun. Call it fate or providence. I met a man who claimed to know what happened the night Ekema and Ozumba switched us. He's been away for a while but has been following my progress since then. When he found out I had been sent to live with your family, he tried to tell your grandfather the truth. Ekema and Ozumba found out what he was up to and tried to kill him, sending him into hiding."

"How did he find you?"

"He's been trying to lure me to come and work for him since I graduated from the university. The night I left, I took a bus to Ajidi and went straight to the address he gave me. He didn't reveal the treachery to me until recently. A few months after I started an apprenticeship in his company, someone informed him that a man who we suspected to be a private investigator was looking for a person by the name Okem. No one knew me by that name. Luckily for me, when I arrived in Ajidi, my benefactor had insisted I go by a different name, which I agreed to, not realizing the plan was for me to remain anonymous. Following that incident with the investigator, he decided it was too dangerous to withhold the truth from me any longer. That was when he told me about the circumstance of my birth."

"The investigator might have been Amah's uncle."

"Why do you say that?"

"I sent Amah's uncle to look for you."

"You tried to look for me?"

"Yes. It was then that the abuse started."

He swallowed hard and paused for a moment.

"I'm so sorry for what you've been through. I'm really sorry I wasn't here to protect you. That has been my biggest regret."

"I wished every second you were here," I said, forcing back tears.

He pondered for a little while as he wiped a tear from the corner of my eye.

"I doubt it was Amah's uncle, though. My benefactor had found whoever was looking for me and paid him handsomely to report the results of his search to him before sharing it with his employer. Amah's uncle wouldn't have been so vile to be playing two sides. So many months passed without results, and the investigator wouldn't reveal who had sent him. When my benefactor thought the coast was clear, he provided some capital for me to start a business and later, land to build a house. My business flourished in no time. I became known as the 'Merchant of Ajidi'."

"Wow! Where is Ekema now? I haven't seen her in a while."

"Still at the palace scheming at all costs for Albert to take the staff, but I heard the staff has eluded him."

"It has. Where could Ozumba be right now?"

"He roams around the palace waiting to take the reins, but he too is in limbo and will remain so if

Albert is unable to grab the staff."

"Did you say limbo? The last time I went to Luenah, Papa revealed Ozumba to me. It completely slipped my mind until now. Ozumba had a wreath on his head. 'A mark of ill will,' my grandfather had said. My grandfather was also trying to tell me something else before I returned."

Okem squeezed my hand excitedly as I spoke. "What was he trying to tell you?"

"I don't know. I regained consciousness before he finished."

He sighed deeply and sank into a chair, my hand still in his.

"Try to recall."

"He was saying something that sounded like 'nothing is what it seems', but he didn't quite finish."

"Ona, try."

"I'm sorry, Okem. That's all there was. I tried really hard to ask Papa about Ozumba, but he wouldn't reveal much."

He slowly let go of my hands and looked up as though he had come to a certain realization.

"Luenah might have the answers we seek. Can you take me to Luenah?" he pleaded.

I grimaced. "I don't think I'm capable of taking someone else to Luenah. I can't even really explain how I get there myself."

"You can if you try. I beg of you—"

"Do you have any clue what you're asking me to

do? It's obvious you don't. Otherwise, you'd know it's impossible."

"Nothing is impossible, my dear," he said as he arose.

"Only *Eris* are allowed into Luenah, Okem. Do you understand that? My grandfather made that very clear to me in the beginning. I think we should start thinking about other options rather than putting all our hopes on Luenah."

"Do you have any other suggestions?"

"I can't think of anything right now, but I'm sure if we put our heads together we can find a viable solution. Give me some time."

"Ona, we don't have time. These people are ruthless, and I'm sure your grandfather can help me. Talk to him on my behalf. Please, I'm begging you."

His eyes were boring through mine.

I tapped my chin as I pondered our predicament. "I'll wait till I get another chance to enter Luenah. One thing you must know is that I have never been able to will myself there. I'll ask my grandfather the next time I see him. What reason should I give him for your wanting to visit?"

"Let him know he needs to show me how to take the staff," he said, breathing heavily.

"Why do you automatically assume he knows how?"

"I can feel it in my bones. Don't ask me how, Ona, because I won't be able to answer. Besides, he disclosed Ozumba and told you he was marked for punishment. What does that tell you? Chances are your grandfather is deeply involved in this. Don't you want to find out how?"

CHAPTER EIGHTEEN

MY HEART WAS heavy when I left the hotel that day. Still in shock from everything I'd just heard, I snuck into my room the moment I got home. I couldn't bear anyone seeing me in that state. None of the servants were around, and Albert wasn't due back for another two days, or else he would have been waiting for me in the parlor. I had all the space I needed to reflect before I meet with Okem the next day. My head hurt as I pondered Okem's request to take him to Luenah. As far as I was concerned, he was asking me to do an impossible thing as I'd never been able to transport myself to Luenah, not for lack of trying but because that skill was beyond the limits of my power. I also didn't see how Luenah could help him, except to gain wisdom and direction. For some reason, Okem believed Luenah would help him make sense of the chaos. The staff was a physical thing. I couldn't fathom how Okem expected Grandfather to help him weather that storm. My thoughts drifted to Albert. If Okem was indeed the Crown Prince, where did that leave Albert? Okem's revelations had left me with more questions than answers. Was Albert really an imposter? Did Albert know? Is that why he hated Okem so much? Did he know where Okem had been all this time? Albert's reaction when he discovered I had asked Amah's uncle to look for Okem now seemed like a terrible red flag. There were many more, and they all flashed through my mind as I pondered Okem's account of the treachery that had gone on right under our noses. I remembered how Ekema doted on Albert. I once told Albert that she loved him like a mother, and he thought that was hilarious. He got along more with Ekema than he did with his own mother, and it all now made sense.

I pulled down the shades, took a long relaxing bath, and changed into a silk robe. With some jazz music playing in the background, I lay on the futon and tried to achieve my next mission — willing myself to Luenah. There were so many critical questions I needed to ask my grandfather, and I needed him to answer all of them this time around. Each time I began to drift away, I found myself jumping back into consciousness. I was unable to relax, let alone concentrate. The book I had been struggling to read for days was staring at me from the side table. I grabbed it and flipped it open to the first page before adjusting the light to avoid straining my eyes. Thirty whole minutes passed, and I neither fell asleep nor drifted into Luenah.

"What if this doesn't work?" I said aloud.

"What if what doesn't work?" I heard someone scoff.

I turned a ninety-degree angle, sending the book on my lap to the ground with a loud thud.

"Albert!"

I jumped right up from the futon, stepping on the book, not caring to retrieve it and wondering how long Albert had been standing there.

"Albert, you're here. I thought you weren't due back for another two days?"

"I canceled my trip. Didn't realize I needed permission from my Queen to do so?" he said half-jokingly.

"No, not at all," I said, shaking my head.

"What did you do with the rest of your day?" he asked. "Did you see Amah?"

"I thought I told you she's traveled to London."

"Oh," he said, smiling wryly.

"I'm glad to see you," I said, taking his hands. At first, it felt reassuring, but little did I know that the smile passing his lips was about to reveal an even bigger monster than the ones he had manifested in the past.

He squeezed my hands tightly.

"Are you really happy to have me back?"

"Yes," I whispered, scared out of my wits.

"How? Happy? Are? You?" he said, still holding both hands tightly, almost as though I was a rag doll. Just as I opened my mouth to speak, everything went dark. Suddenly, I felt something kicking my legs. I struggled to open my eyes and there was Albert.

"Tell me again how much you've missed me. Did you miss me when you were with Okem?" He was yelling.

I opened my mouth again to speak, but nothing came forth.

"You can't speak because you were with Okem," he continued to berate me.

I gasped.

"Did you think I wouldn't find out about your little secret? Huh? You take men to a hotel because that's the type of person you are. You are nothing without me."

Stunned to find myself on the ground and unable to recall how I got there, I felt something dripping into my mouth. With my index finger, I patted my nose. It was tender and blood was on my hand.

"You should go with that nonentity," he concluded, hissing and walking out the door.

I waited till the sound of his footsteps faded before I walked to the bathroom and looked at myself in the mirror. My nose was still bleeding, and one side of my face was swollen. As I ran the tap and wondered how pathetic I had become, my mind ran to Okem. He was in danger. I had to get to him.

Okem

Right after Ona left my room at the Palisir hotel, I pondered for long everything that was going on. Unable to think properly indoors, I decided to take a walk around the hotel grounds to clear my head. An hour later, I came back upstairs to take a nap as I hadn't slept the night before. I lay down on the sofa and thought about all the things I'd discussed with Ona since my return. They had thrown me off course. I couldn't help but think that if I hadn't been so hot-headed, I would have waited to hear everything she had to say the day I left. Even now, Ona's grandfather's words come back to me. "Okem, you need to calm down sometimes and listen," he'd always say. They are almost prophetic, and I wished I listened then. But there's no need crying over spilled milk. I remember when I used to sit down with him and eat *akara* and *akamu*. Oh, how I've missed him. Almost as much as I've missed Ona. I wish everything could go back to the way it was. If only I could turn back the hands of time and make things right. But how can I make things better? God please, make this pain go away. That snake Albert is ruining her life. The mere fact that he's in it is interrupting her whole existence. He's always been wrong for her, and because of him, she's just roaming the earth without a purpose.

Just as those last thoughts crossed my mind, my heart sank, and I lost touch with my surroundings. Before I knew it, I found myself walking down a narrow path, bordered by trees on both sides and streams of water flowing beneath. Confused as to how I got there, I turned around to retrace my steps. All I saw were images of wild creatures in varying shapes and sizes, representing doom and gloom. I continued on my path, with longer strides this time, praying the creatures behind me would disappear. As I began to calm down and appreciate the tranquility offered by the trail in front of me, I reached its tail end and floated into another reality.

"I told Ona the same thing." I heard a deep voice say.

The moment my eyes collided with the striking figure before me, I realized I was looking at Ona's grandfather. He'd changed a bit, but I was certain it was him.

"I made it clear to Ona," he continued, "that the person she marries will either propel or thwart her purpose on earth."

"Where am I?" I asked, confused. I thought I'd died and woken up in heaven. I marveled at the beautiful surroundings, the mountains, the rivers, the lush vegetation, and the life forms. Everything seemed so familiar and yet so strange.

"You've finally made it," Ona's grandfather declared.

"This is Luenah?" I stuttered, still aghast.

"That's right."

"I've been dreaming of this place for years. No wonder the times Ona described it to me, it felt like somewhere I'd been before. Now I understand why. I have been here. I am so sure now. This must be how you found me, Sir."

"We've been waiting a long time for you," Ona's grandfather said.

A carriage pulled up right in front of us, and he took my hand to lead me in.

"My son," he said. "This is a great feat. Congratulations. Only a select few make it to Luenah. You're one of the chosen ones. You're one of the few in the long line of *Eris*."

* * *

We rode for what seemed like a whole day to the shrine. It was a marvelous ride. I don't believe Ona did it justice when she described it to me many years ago. On entering the shrine, the whole court sat quietly as though they had been anticipating my visit.

The throne room was filled to the brim, and there seemed to be some sort of celebration going on. A feast was spread out. The man I assumed to be the supreme ruler of Luenah was on the throne. He was resplendent in a long gilded robe that swept the floor beneath him. The late King—the *Ideme*, my father— was there too. He held a heavy object in his hand. I bowed before him.

"Father?" I said, sighing deeply.

"My son."

"Father."

"Son, I am so sorry that I wasn't able to protect you on earth. Please forgive me. I was only human. My only consolation is that the infinite being was there for you."

"I'm sorry too, Father. What they did to you was evil. They deprived you of your offspring."

"Don't worry, my son. Everything happens for a reason. The most important thing is that the wrongs will be made right, and the truth will be revealed soon."

"How? There's been so much damage. And who will believe me?"

"They will have no choice but to believe you after you leave here today. You will have the blessing and the anointing you need."

He stretched out his hand to further reveal the object he was holding.

"With this," he said, "no one can come between

you and your destiny."

I froze to the spot as I stared at the twenty-inch-long wooden structure, detailed with brass tacks. The top part depicted a man's head with elaborate headgear and scarification marks on the face. The handle was twisted, had a separate ring at the top, with pyro-engraved details.

"The staff," I finally muttered and shifted my gaze to my father and then back to the precious gift he held in his hand.

"Take it, my son. It is yours."

I stretched out both hands and took the staff. I examined it with admiration, a smile spreading across my face, and joy filling my heart.

"Thank you, Father. I didn't know it would be this easy to take this staff."

The late King nodded and chuckled lightly.

"Yes, it's that easy. You see, this heirloom is not a physical thing. It's spiritual. What those hooligans didn't know was that they couldn't just pick it up from its sanctuary just because they stole your birthright. The staff cannot be transferred from person to person indiscriminately. It is rightfully yours. Take good care of it and everything it represents and then pass it on to your heir—your first-born child. You will know when the time is right. I had tried to pass it to Albert, but I couldn't because it wasn't rightfully his. The spoilt brat doesn't even know it, but he is finished."

"Did Albert know the staff wasn't his?"

The *Ideme* shook his head. "But he will soon find out. He is being told of his legacy as we speak."

"So he was an innocent victim like me?"

The late King hesitated a bit before saying, "He was at birth, but unfortunately, with parents like Ozumba and Ekema, what chance did he have to remain pure? Ekema had a great influence on him. He was her puppet."

"How do I carry the staff out of Luenah?" I asked, looking around at the faces in the throne room.

The entire court laughed. I laughed too, not knowing why everyone thought my question was funny but happy to be in the company of friends.

The *Ideme* cut through the laughter.

"I guess you haven't figured it out by yourself. Here it is: anything you bind in the spirit will be bound there on earth. Everything in this world, including creation itself, was first manifested in the spirit before it transcended in the multi-dimensional world you live in. Go now. When you arrive, the staff will disappear from your hand, but you will be able to pick it up from the sanctuary with no trouble. No one on earth has the power to do that but you."

"Thank you, sir," I said, bowing again to him.

"Thank you, Father would be more appropriate. Now go in peace and take what already belongs to you. I don't promise that it will be easy, but as long as you pursue it with courage, you will come out victorious."

I drifted back to earth before I could respond. It took me a while to regain consciousness and realize where I was. When I finally came around, I jumped right up and looked around the room in confusion. That was when I heard Ona's frantic knock on the door and her voice calling, "Okem open for me!"

Ona

The moment Albert left my room, I ran out of the house, went straight to the garage, and got into my car. The guards banged on the window and made signs for me to step out of the car, but I ignored them and drove straight to the Palisir hotel. I doubt they had heard the squabble in my room, but they must have seen Albert drive off in a hurry. On my way, I struggled to catch my breath. I couldn't believe what had just happened. I had been afraid of Albert for far too long. Now that I had the chance to face the fear of his assault, I felt stronger and more confident than ever. I tried to call Okem from the lobby, and when he didn't respond, I took the elevator to room 765 to meet him. His jaw clenched, and his chest heaved up and down as a combination of pain or anger clouded his face as he opened the door and removed the scarf I'd used to disguise the bruises on my face.

"Ona, don't tell me Albert did this to you?"

Asides from my swollen eyes, Albert's hand had created impressions all over my face, my arms, and my shoulders. The bleeding in my nose had subsided, but it was raw and swollen.

"Okem, Albert knows you're around. He found out that I came here."

"Is that why he did this? And how did he find out where you were?"

"I don't know. I'm not sure how I blew my cover," I said, staring at him. "You need to get out of here! After what you told me earlier, there's no telling what Albert will do if he finds out your exact location. He already knows you're here at the Palisir."

"Don't worry," Okem said as he lifted me off the ground and placed me gently on the large bed. "I'll call my men immediately to find me another place to stay, but please try to remain calm now."

He walked swiftly to the bathroom and emerged with a damp towel, which he folded and placed on my jaw. "I have to take you to the hospital. This cold compress should calm the swelling until you can see a doctor."

"Is it that bad?" I grunted.

"I can't believe you just asked that. You sound like you've gotten used to this treatment. Your entire face is swollen, and the white in one eye is red. Yes.

It's that bad."

"It hurts so much," I said, running my hand across my face.

"From now on, you should never be alone with that guy. This nonsense should end now."

"It's already over."

"Is it?" he asked, glaring at me.

"Believe me, Okem. It's over!"

He paused for a few moments and let out a sigh before continuing. "Can you believe that I was just about to phone you before I heard you knock?"

"Really?"

"Yes. I wanted to tell you that I went there. It was unbelievable. I've never seen anything so amazing," he said, moving the towel from my jaw to my right cheek, while I stared at him in silence.

"Where? You went where?"

"Where else? Luenah!"

"That's not possible," I said, attempting to sit up on the bed. He held my shoulder to stop me.

"Nothing is impossible, my dear."

"I don't dispute that. It's just that I can't believe we get to share this experience. I just can't believe it. Did you see Papa?"

"Yes. And my father, the *Ideme*. He was there too. I came back with more questions than answers, though."

"What did you find out?"

"Your eye," he said, a look of concern covering

his face. "The swelling is increasing. Let's leave now!"
He reached out to take my hand.

"Something you told me earlier doesn't add up
though," I said, letting him pull me up gently from
the bed. "The man in Ajidi…your benefactor, why
didn't he report the incident after he escaped?"

"Ona, don't you know how things work around
here?"

"I'm not sure I know what you mean."

"Well, it was too dangerous. I found out later
that these people—Ozumba and Ekema—control the
Special Security Forces in the region. They also head
the cabal responsible for most of the ills plaguing our
society today. They have spread their evil tentacles
everywhere, bribing to get their way into every corner
of authority. To satisfy their greed, they pay those
youths to clash and cause confusion, while they
benefit from the spoils. Following these clashes, they
accumulate large masses of land for themselves,
which they end up holding to create artificial scarcity.
In the end, they sell the amassed lands at ridiculous
prices and under different fake names to conceal their
connection to the scheme. You see, he couldn't report
the issue. He didn't think anyone would believe him.
And without adequate proof, he would have been
thrown into jail and murdered for even daring to
come up with such a 'ridiculous' accusation."

"I understand. His hands were tied."

"Very much so."

"Something is still bothering me. We still don't have a way of proving you're the *Ideme's* son. What should we do?"

"When we heard the King had died and Albert, his heir couldn't lift the staff, everything my benefactor had been trying to say to me fell into place. Not that I didn't believe him before then. The striking resemblance I bore to the *Ideme* was all the proof I needed to know he was my father."

"Why didn't you come back then?"

"I would have. My benefactor made arrangements for me to come back, but when the clashes and the human sacrifices started occurring, it became extremely dangerous for me to expose the crime without a rock-solid plan."

"Do you have a rock-solid plan now?"

"I do."

"What is it?"

Until now, I'd never thought the plan would involve you until you mentioned seeing Ozumba in Luenah. I have more than a plan now. I have the power to take the staff. I took it in Luenah."

"You did?" I screeched, grabbing his shoulders with both hands.

He nodded slowly. "I did."

I hugged him with my aching body and kissed him softly on the lips. As I held onto him, I could hear his heart pounding loudly in his chest. Tears were beginning to well up in my eyes again. This time it was tears of joy.

"What do we do now?" I whispered after a few minutes had passed.

He released me and looked into my eyes. Seeing the tear running down my cheek aroused his sentimental side.

"Oh, Ona, don't cry. You're safe now. I'll never let anyone hurt you again. I promise."

"I know, Okem. I'm just happy. But what should we do now? Where do we go from here?"

"We just have to find a way to convince the kingmakers to let me into the sanctuary to pick up the staff."

"Just like that?"

"I know people that can help," he said rather confidently.

"I pray it all works out, and I hope Ekema and Ozumba are exposed and punished to the fullest extent of the law."

"I do not doubt that they will be," he said, shaking his head. "Get your shoes and let's go to the hospital."

"Okay but just a second. I'd like to use the bathroom."

CHAPTER NINETEEN

TWO MINUTES AFTER I entered the bathroom, I heard a loud banging on the door.

"Ona, please stay there until I figure out what's going on," Okem said to me.

"Who's there?" he yelled.

The banging continued as Okem opened the door. Curious, I peered through the bathroom door and saw Albert standing there with the signature crease on his forehead. His jaw was clenched. His eyes were bloodshot, and his mouth quivered with such intensity that I feared he would have a seizure. I gently crept back into the bathroom, hoping he hadn't seen me, and then stood in front of the mirror, pondering my next move.

"What do you want?" Okem asked, resisting the urge to punch Albert in the face.

He slithered past Okem and walked into the room.

"I know Ona is your friend. I've taken care of her, but she constantly disappoints me."

"I know how you've taken care of her," Okem countered. "That's how a man takes care of a woman. That's how your father took care of your mother."

"Shut your mouth. I'm a king." Albert was yelling.

"King of fools. You're nobody's king."

"Are you crazy?"

I had heard enough. I opened the bathroom door and stepped out. Albert turned around, and when he saw me, he shook his head before looking at Okem, and then at me, again.

"Oh. So, this is where you ran to," he said in an arrogant tone. "I see you haven't learned your lesson."

"Why don't you teach me that lesson," Okem interjected.

He ignored Okem and walked towards me.

"I can't believe you," he said, grabbing my hand so tight, it hurt. "One minute, you're the esteemed fiancée of the Crown Prince of Ide and the next you're a common tart. You were this close," he said, pressing his thumb against his index finger, "to being a respectfully married woman, and now you've blown it by hiding out in this...this man's hotel room. I should have known you would run here."

His voice was heavy, slurred by anger or alcohol, or both, I couldn't tell.

"Let go of me," I yelled.

He ignored me and started to pull with a kind of ferocious intensity, attempting to drag me out of the room.

"Leave her alone!" Okem demanded.

"Or what will happen? You idiot!"

"I said, leave her alone," Okem repeated, approaching us. "For once in your life pick on somebody your size."

To Albert, it was like a spark that ignited the keg of powder that he was. That was when he pulled out a revolver and aimed it at Okem.

"You seriously think I'll let you keep my fiancée? *Eh?* Which alternate universe did you both arrive from?" he yelled and waved his gun dangerously at both of us."

"Put the gun down," Okem ordered, gesturing with both hands in Albert's general direction.

Albert ignored him and fired a shot at the television. The bullet made a hole through the glass, and fumes gushed out of the screen. I was frozen to the spot, unable to cry or scream.

"Call the police," Okem whispered to me.

"If you move," Albert said, pointing the gun in my direction, "I need not tell you what will happen to you. Do I?"

I stared at Albert and then at the gun. It was

pointing right at my head.

"Albert, you'll shoot me?" I asked, choking on my words.

"Without regret."

My head reeled as I fell slowly to the ground. I remembered Okem's visit to Luenah, and that gave me strength. Okem was destined to take the staff and nothing, no one on earth could stop him. Soon, I lost touch with my surroundings and slowly drifted away into slight unconsciousness. I thought I was about to die. As I prayed for my grandfather to come and rescue me, I was jolted by the sound of a quarrel, and I moved my legs slowly, trying to get up.

Albert got distracted by my movements, and Okem ran towards him and tried to grab the gun from his hand. They wrestled before the pistol fell to the ground, making a loud crashing noise as it let out fire on impact. I was so frightened I felt as though my heart would stop. I crawled as fast as I could to reach the gun, but Albert was faster than the rest of us. Okem lunged at him, and they struggled for a few seconds before I heard a loud pop. I screamed, not knowing which of the men, Albert or Okem had pulled the trigger.

Albert dropped the gun and sank to his knees, grabbing his throat with both hands, a wild look registering on his face.

I ran to his side in terror while Okem got on the phone with the police. While we waited, I grabbed a sheet and held it against his neck to prevent excessive blood loss. Hotel security, having been alerted by the three gunshots, stormed into the room. Okem's driver, Albert's security team, and hotel guests crowded the door, almost causing a stampede. It was an excruciating fifteen minutes before the ambulance drove Albert to the hospital. He had lost a lot of blood and was barely conscious when the paramedics arrived at the scene. My pleas to accompany him fell on deaf ears as they denied me entry into the van.

* * *

The policemen drove us to the police station in their car. Okem and I were taken to different rooms and interrogated for hours. I still had Albert's blood on my skin and my clothes, and I was drained from hunger and exhaustion. After answering their questions the best I could, I felt battered and beaten in the end. It was not until close to midnight that I saw Okem again. His driver drove us to the hospital where the doctor, having been previously alerted about the incident at the hotel, asked his staff to wheel me to the examination room immediately. After a thorough assessment, the doctor kept me under observation for another hour. By the time Okem drove me home after two in the morning, there was nothing left of me. There was also nothing left for us to do. Just the dreaded talk with my grandmother to explain to her what had been going on.

* * *

As expected, news over the airwaves had alerted my grandmother of the happenings that day, so she was waiting anxiously for me by the time I got home. Despite my state, she gave me a long hug. Ifedi was standing behind her.

"Ona, what caused all of this?" my grandmother asked, her voice broken to the core. I could tell she had been crying. "How are you? Look at your face."

I sighed. "Grandma, Okem will fill you in."

"Yes. Ifedi told me Okem was back. Is he the cause of all this?"

I shook my head. "As I said, he'll fill you in. Can I be excused? I need to rid myself of this stench," I said, pointing at my bloody clothes. "Okem will soon come in. He's outside, giving some instructions to his driver. I'll join you after I get a thorough wash."

"Okay! We'll wait for you."

I left for my bedroom, and Ifedi, who hadn't uttered a word since I stepped in, followed me closely behind.

"Ona, what did you say happened?"

"I don't have the energy to talk now. I'm in so much pain. I was hoping Okem will do the talking for me."

"Okay. Will you like me to help you with your bath?"

"No thank you. I'll be fine."

She followed me into my room regardless and watched as I stepped into the bathroom and shut the door behind me. Relieved to be alone, I poured a generous portion of my lemon-infused bubble bath in the tub. The sharp fragrance was strong without being overpowering. I filled the tub with water to about the half-way mark, ripped off all my clothes, and threw them into a disposal bag. After settling in, I scrubbed my skin until it almost blistered. Satisfied that I had cleansed all of Albert's blood from my person, I pulled out the stopper for the water to run out. It made a loud gurgling noise as the liquid rearranged itself to escape from the drain. With the showerhead, I rinsed the excess soap from my body. The feeling of the sprinkles on my skin got me to relax for the first time that evening until I recalled Okem and my grandmother would be waiting for me. I got out of the bathroom and dried myself with a towel, threw on the nightgown and housecoat Ifedi had neatly placed at the bottom of my bed, and ran downstairs to meet them.

Out the window, the sky was pitch-black except for a few twinkling stars. The security lights that defined the homes in the valley were in full glow. Okem was seated silently when I got into the living room. Ifedi was standing near the door, and my grandmother was looking rather agitated, bobbing her leg, and sighing at intervals as she asked a barrage of questions: "Okem, where have you been?

Why did you run away? Were you that angry with us?"

"Something was happening in my head. I just needed to get away," Okem responded.

"Something that bad?"

As I got closer, the room seemed to be getting smaller, about to crush me. I collapsed into a chair and reminded myself to breathe.

"I was just briefing Mama," Okem said.

"Ona, your face," Ifedi shrieked. "I didn't notice how bad it was earlier."

"Let me see," my grandmother said, edging her seat closer to mine.

"Heavenly Father!" she screamed. "What happened to you?"

I was hoping she wouldn't notice my face in the dimly lit room. Now that Ifedi had called her attention to it, I would have to go into more detail than I needed to. But all I wanted to do was retire for the night.

"I can't believe you allowed things to get to this point," my grandmother continued, glaring at me. "Albert is your fiancé. What were you doing in that hotel room with Okem, and why are you not by Albert's side?"

"Grandma. Hasn't Okem told you?"

"Told me what?"

"I was just about to tell her the whole story before you came in," Okem said.

"Okay. I'm listening," my grandmother sighed, pausing halfway to grab the hem of her wrapper. "What you're about to tell me had better explain this mess or someone will pay. Ifedi, thank you so much for everything. You can go to bed now. Close that door behind you. I'll turn off the lights when we're done."

"Okay Ma, goodnight."

"Okay, my dear. Do you know Ifedi has been running around the whole city trying to find out where you were, Ona?" my grandmother said, turning abruptly to face me after Ifedi had left. "First, she ran to the hotel, then to the police station and then to the hospital where she was refused entry because a crowd had gathered there. Albert was taken to the same hospital and the masses had kept a vigil for him. I was about to run there myself before a nurse at the hospital called me to confirm that you had been discharged and were on your way home. Have you seen the kind of trouble you put me through?"

"I'm sorry Grandma."

"*Ngwa*, okay, begin. Tell me what happened."

I had never seen my grandmother so angry. I believed her threats, so I garnered the last ounce of strength in me to remain there. Okem and I took turns and explained everything to her. We started from Albert's initial assault and all the things that happened afterwards and ended with the incident at the hotel. Next, we told her Okem's story, starting from when Okem was exchanged at birth until his return. We carefully left out Luenah. My grandmother was already in so much shock. Luenah would have tipped the scale. As I spoke, she grabbed hold of me and pulled me close.

"I thought Albert was going to kill me," I concluded, holding her shoulders to calm her down.

"God forbid." She said, snapping her fingers before she placed both hands on her head and crashed to the floor. "*Chai! Uwammebioo,* this world is coming to an end."

I took her hand and pleaded with her to get up. She finally budged and sat on the chair.

"What do we do now?" she said, looking at Okem.

"Certain moves will need to be made to right old wrongs, but until we've concluded the steps I need to carry out with the kingmakers, we cannot breathe a word about this to anybody."

"No problem," she said, hissing and shaking her head. "I'm too tired. I need to go to bed."

"Okay, Ma," Okem replied and helped her upstairs to her bedroom. On the way, he consoled her and wiped her tears.

"Ona, I'm so sorry," Okem said after he returned to the parlor.

"Why?"

"I feel responsible for all this pain."

"You're not to blame, Okem. Albert is

responsible for this evening."

"I don't know."

"Okem, I'm so scared."

"There's no need to be scared," he assured me, reaching out for a hug.

"We could have died tonight. Our lives could have ended."

"Let me take you to your room. You need your rest."

* * *

Safely in my room, I sat on the bed, and Okem walked to the balcony. He spread a mat on the floor and invited me to lie beside him. The light outside had since disappeared, so we lay down silently, gazing at the star-lit sky.

"This reminds me of those days we used to sleep out here on hot evenings," Okem said to break the silence. "Those were the good old days."

"Before my grandma thought it was dangerous for us to be so close to each other."

He laughed.

I turned to look at his face. His silhouette and the mere fact that he was right there caused my heart to skip a beat. He turned and smiled before grabbing my chin and kissing me tenderly on the lips.

"I love you," he said.

"I love you, too."

We lay face to face in the dark, listening to the

sound of each other's breathing and taking in each aspect as though the world could end right then.

"Do you think your grandmother will be okay?" Okem asked after a while.

"She will be," I said, after pondering for a second. She's been the head of this family for a while, so she knows how to handle tough situations."

"I hope she understands that she has to let me handle this one. It's such a complicated affair."

"I think she does," I responded.

"I'm curious. Why did you avoid any mention of your grandfather or Luenah to her?"

"Oh, that? Would she have been able to handle it? I don't think so. I'll eventually tell her. There's an unwritten rule in this house: no-one talks about Papa. I'm lucky that I get to see him once in a while in Luenah, otherwise, can you imagine how miserable I would have been?"

"If you had shared your experience with your grandmother, it would have helped with her healing too."

"I disagree."

"Well." He shrugged. "You have to tell her at some point."

"I will, but I can't help thinking about Albert. I hope he recovers soon."

"I hope so, too," Okem said. "I feel sorry for him, but when I consider that he may have come to the Palisir hotel to kill me or even you, I feel relieved."

"That is so true. Albert may not have been part of this conspiracy from the get-go, but he became lethal to our existence the moment he found out he was an impostor."

I shivered. The wind had suddenly become cold.

"Let me take you inside." Okem offered.

* * *

Soon after Okem left, I slipped under my covers and lay down for hours on end ruminating on the eventful day we had. The horror of Albert's wound was enough to rob me of sleep for a whole month. There was no way of knowing what would happen from then on, and what would happen to Albert. Would he live or die?

CHAPTER TWENTY

IT'D BEEN TWO weeks since Albert received that bullet wound on his neck. Two weeks since he'd been in intensive care. Two weeks since he gave me those dirty slaps that sent me running to the Palisir. Yet it seemed like yesterday. The surgical procedure to remove the bullet from his neck left him unconscious. Although he'd bruised and abused me, I prayed day and night for his recovery but swore to never live with him as man and wife. Okem was back, and he was all I ever needed. My years of dreaming and hoping were over. The kingmakers were carrying out a secret investigation into the allegations that Okem and Albert were switched at birth. It didn't matter if Okem turned out not to be the rightful heir to the throne because nothing would make me turn my back on him. Nothing would make me ever lose sight of him again.

Our lives became chaotic from then on. When we were not at the police station, the police were swarming our space to repeat the process of interrogation over and over again. Okem and I were exhausted from the badgering, and then the fear set in. What if Albert recovered and tried to implicate us? What if he kidnapped me and forced my hand in marriage? What if he had hired assassins before his accident to kill Okem? The questions were endless, and I started to doubt myself again.

The situation made it impossible for us to make plans for our future. As Albert battled for his life, Ekema, whose influence we were sure kept us within the police radar, tormented us. She barged into Grandma's house late one evening and demanded to see Okem. From my position in the study, I could hear them fairly well as she confronted him in the parlor.

"I will make life miserable for you," she swore.

"Why? What did I do to deserve a miserable life?"

"What did you do? My son—my nephew is lying in the hospital because of you, and you're acting as though you don't know what I'm talking about."

She had let the cat out of the bag. The moment she said my son and then corrected it to nephew, I confirmed everything Okem had told me about her. It was sad that Okem couldn't confront her with the truth right away, but I was impressed by his extraordinary composure.

"It's an accident, Ma."

"Don't call me, Ma. I'm not your Ma," Ekema said in an exasperated tone.

"Okay, Aunty."

"I'm not your Aunty either," she said, raising her hand in warning. "Don't call me that either."

I struggled to stifle a giggle. I wondered if Okem called her aunty to see if he could elicit a bigger reaction from her. We had discussed the importance of maintaining discretion regarding everything he had told me about Ekema as it was dangerous to reveal things before the kingmakers had finished their investigation. Laying accusations without lining up all the areas of the defense against someone in her position could be dangerous. At the minimum, she could sue for libel. At worst, our lives could be jeopardized. Okem had pleaded with me to be patient. He needed a little more time to sort things out properly. I was running out of patience, though. With Ekema's reputation, I feared that she might try again to eliminate Okem. Any hint that her actions were getting close to being exposed and that risk could go over the roof. Add the fact that her only child was stuck to a hospital bed, and we may have one evil, irrational human being on our hands.

"I can't believe how calm you were," I said to Okem after Ekema left. "Are you sure we shouldn't take this issue up right now? You know she could hit again before you finalize your plan."

"We're on track, my dear. A little bird told me Ekema goes to the hospital every day to visit Albert, and she sleeps there most nights. She hasn't got any time to plot. Besides, we're not behind on our plans. The kingmakers will be communing by the end of the week."

"I heard her threatening to lock you up. What if she succeeds before the kingmakers finish their investigation?"

"Ekema's threats won't hold up anywhere. You already know that. Several witnesses saw Albert banging on my hotel door that fateful afternoon. The police interviewed each of them, and their statements matched our own account. Also, don't forget that the gun was registered in Albert's name, and his hand, not mine, had traces of gunpowder. It's obvious what happened was an accident."

"I can't wait for all of this to be over."

"Me neither," Okem said, shaking his head.

"Albert's statement is the only thing required to close the police inquiry," I reminded him.

"I pray when he eventually regains consciousness and is able to speak, he'll do the right thing and put an end to this madness."

"Only God knows what Albert will do. The guy is full of surprises."

* * *

I hadn't been to Luenah in a while, and with all that was going on, I felt bare without its influence. The last time I was there, my grandfather had mentioned that nothing was ever as it seemed. I had confirmed that to be absolutely true, just like all his other predictions. All the same, something didn't sit right with me. How did Papa become entangled in all of this? And what could it possibly have to do with my purpose? I had been groomed to be queen, and there I was queen-in-waiting to two men, one lying unconscious in the hospital, and the other at a crossroads, waiting for the decision of the kingmakers. Neither man had taken the staff in real life, although one not for lack of trying.

One quiet afternoon, a feeling of restlessness overcame me, so I walked around my room, arranging and rearranging my closet as I hummed a tune. Next, I cleaned my bathtub which had received a thorough cleaning by one of the servants earlier that day. I was willing to do anything to keep myself from thinking about the issues that were constantly cropping up in my head. I wished to be in Luenah more than anything else, as I pondered what my personal truth could be. Rather than wait to be summoned, I lay on the settee and tested the limits of my power. A familiar force erupted inside my chest, pulling me with as much intensity as I ventured towards it. My feet had found the narrow path to

Luenah. The sun was bright and high up in the sky, unlike the pitch darkness I experienced one of the times I was there. I reached the tail end of the path and sauntered into Luenah. To my surprise, rather than the seashore, I found myself atop a hill overlooking a wide stretch of fields. The shrine was in the distance, its resplendence in full view, an assault on the senses. I swathed a bee off my face. The sun's rays on the rolling hills caused the tips to sparkle like gemstones. While I admired the sheer beauty of my surroundings, my grandfather stepped out of the carriage about three yards away from me. Excited to see him, I ran down the hill and entered with glee.

"Congratulations on making it to Luenah by yourself. You completely let go of doubt, and your *chi* agreed with you."

"Thank you, Papa. I never knew this was at all possible. Had I known, I would have come earlier."

"Now, you must have come for a reason. What do you seek?"

I went straight to the point and asked him what had been plaguing my mind.

"Why you, Papa?"

He paused a little.

"Coming to live with me was no coincidence, and neither was Okem's."

"Why Okem?"

"Don't you see why already? Our destinies are intertwined. And by our, I mean all three of us."

"I can see that now. But, I also feel you're still withholding something from me."

"You're right. I'm still withholding some things, but I had to wait for the right time to tell you everything."

"Everything?"

"Yes. It's time, but before I do, I need you to promise that you will act with wisdom in getting the issues resolved the proper way."

"I promise to do as you ask, Papa."

"For starters, how do you think I left the earth?"

"If I recall correctly, I didn't see you before I left for school that day as I usually did, and that upset me a little. By the time I came back, they told me you never woke up from sleep the night before, and I was devastated. That was when I found out you had passed overnight."

"That's right. I was already dying when you and I sat at dinner the night before. They poisoned me."

My head turned suddenly as my bewildered gaze searched his face.

"They? Poison? Who?" I muttered.

My grandfather nodded his head slowly.

"I'm here today and not on earth with you because of Ozumba and Ekema. Together, they plotted to take my life, and they succeeded. However, they would not have been able to do that without the help of someone very strategic in the household. Think about this. Ozumba and Ekema had no access to me, I had never met Ekema, and I never saw Ozumba after the day he brought Okem to live with us—"

"What are you saying, Papa? That someone else was involved? There were only five of us in the house that day: me, you, Okem, Grandma, and Ifedi."

"There you go,"

I was aghast.

"Papa, please don't scare me."

"It was Ifedi."

"Ifedi? Don't tell me that, Papa. Are you saying Ifedi is a murderer?"

"Yes. She was right in the middle of it."

"Oh my God," I screamed, feeling confused.

"That might be the hardest part for you to believe, but that is the truth. Unknowingly to your grandmother and me, Ifedi came to serve at our house through a reference Ekema had provided. Ifedi was carefully instated in our home to help them carry out their evil schemes."

I heard my heart thumping in my chest as I listened to my grandfather. At first, everything he was saying to me sounded implausible. But as so many thoughts crossed my mind, and I recalled that Ifedi had come to live with us right about the time Okem moved in, a shiver ran through my spine.

"She administered the poison that killed me," my grandfather continued.

I coughed to clear the congestion that suddenly

built up in my throat.

"No... no... no..." I placed my hand on my chest. It was suddenly so hard to breathe. "Papa, did you say Ifedi?"

He nodded.

I bit my lips so hard they began to bleed.

"You should be careful from now on. And don't act so stunned. The people closest to you could also turn out to be your greatest enemies. Look at Okem, his aunty, his blood, tried to steal his birthright. She would have killed him if she had the power. Anointed blood would have been spilled, and she would have run mad if she dared. I believe she knew that. Otherwise, Okem would not be alive today. What she didn't know was that his life was not the only thing out of bounds to her, but the staff was too. She underestimated its power."

"Why didn't you tell me earlier, Papa. About Ifedi. I was in mortal danger."

My grandfather shook his head.

"She would not have been able to harm you."

"How? She was with me every day. She had the opportunity to do whatever she may have wanted to do with me all these years. If she could murder you, then she certainly could have done the same to me." I shuddered as I spoke.

"She was part of the equation of your life. It would have done no good if I had revealed this to you earlier. Sometimes these things are allowed to happen for no apparent reason other than for us to grow. If someone really close to you has never hurt you to the depths of humanity, then you wouldn't believe such treachery was possible. This lesson is very important in your new role, the one you've been prepared for. Many will cluster around and try to befriend you. Be careful of the 'wolves in sheep's clothing'."

"Do you think the path is clear now, Papa? Can I face the reality of this type of betrayal now?"

"Absolutely, my dear. God is faithful. The truth only comes to us when we have acquired all the skills needed to confront the hard realities the revelation of such a betrayal brings with it. Knowing the truth alone would not have saved you if you did not have the courage required to deal with it. The same courage that drove you to me in Luenah will take your pain from this betrayal and translate it into action."

"Papa, this is torture. Ifedi may have killed you physically, but she killed my soul with her betrayal. What do you call this pain I feel in my heart? Does everyone have someone close betray them this much?"

My grandfather shook his head and smiled.

"No. Not only are you *Eri*, but also, you've been earmarked for greatness. You will be Queen. In that position, you're considered the most important woman in the kingdom, so you needed that lesson.

Only a handful of people in this world will experience that magnitude of betrayal—only the ones with a big mission to accomplish. You should consider yourself lucky. You were in the raw before now, and just like any precious stone after its rough edge has been polished, you're now ready to get on the journey to occupy your purpose."

"It's all making sense now."

"You see," he continued, "I found out what Ozumba and Ekema were up to, and I was planning to take Okem to his father that weekend and reveal their treachery, but Ifedi found out and informed her accomplices. How she discovered my plans, I don't know, because I didn't breathe a word of it to anybody, not even to your grandmother. Back then, I had told you Okem was to travel with me for a few days, and all Ifedi and your grandmother knew was that preparations were being made for Okem to accompany me on a business trip to Ajidi. Ifedi put the poison in the jug of palm wine your grandmother always leaves me after dinner."

"*Tufiakwa*," I said, snapping my fingers like my grandmother always did whenever she heard something dreadful. My stomach was in knots, and tears streamed down my face. "What should I do now, Papa?"

"The first step is for you to accept your reality. Once you've done that, you'll find it easier to fight your personal battles. Go! I believe you have everything you need to handle this situation. Trust your instincts. Have the courage to do what they ask of you because they'll always lead you to the truth."

CHAPTER TWENTY-ONE

I REGAINED CONSCIOUSNESS soon after my grandfather vanished. The news I just received left my body in a near dormant state. What treachery I have endured! I imagined how shocked Ifedi and her cohorts must have been when Albert and I first started dating. Our meeting in Ajidi so far away from home was one of those fatalistic inevitabilities that made me realize my position as the future Queen was part of my destiny. The same meeting played the role of bringing Albert and Okem together. I shivered as I thought about the magnitude of the danger Okem was in at the moment. Again, he was within the radar of his pursuers. I imagined their panic when he appeared out of the blue after they thought they'd heard the last of him.

Still in shock, I played our life with Ifedi over

and over in my mind searching for any clues I may have missed. The red flags were everywhere. I recalled the conversation I had with Ifedi the day Okem disappeared from our lives. Her body language had been urging me to say more when she knew Okem was listening. She likely knew it would help their course if Okem were to be as far away from Ide as possible. It now made sense why she was always so protective of Albert knowing full well it was Okem I loved. She had never been nice to Okem in the past, but her attitude towards him had worsened around the time Albert came into my life. That was about the time she made it clear to everyone that cared to listen that Okem was the help. This left me confused at the time. As I began to recall the events leading up to the confrontation at the Palisir hotel, my conviction increased. There was no doubt in my mind that Ifedi had alerted Albert about Okem's return. If not, how did Albert suddenly cancel his trip and appear in my room that fateful afternoon?

My heart palpitated the more I thought about all the scenarios. Evidence of Ifedi's treachery was everywhere. They were subtle, but the pieces of the puzzle fit perfectly together. It was still hard to believe she was capable of the things my grandfather accused her of. Had the news been from a source other than my grandfather, I would not have considered even listening. Grandpa had left the resolution to me. He seemed so sure that I would know how to handle it. In my state, there was only one thing I felt I could do—hand her over to the authorities. Hopefully, she would confess and make things easy for everyone. But first, I needed to alert my grandmother.

* * *

I sauntered into my grandmother's room after I made a slight recovery from the news I just received, or so I thought. There must have been remnants of shock on my face because the moment I opened the door, I heard her say, "Ona, what is it? You look like you just saw a ghost."

After I told her everything I knew about Ifedi's betrayal, she wrapped her arms around herself and shook like a leaf. She was rattled and speechless for a few minutes while I stared out of the window waiting for her to regain her composure.

"What is this Luenah?" she kept asking after she'd heard me mention it a few times.

I couldn't keep it a secret any longer. I painstakingly explained my mystical world and confessed to being transported there sometimes to meet Grandfather or to discover things on my own.

"Now, I've heard everything there is to hear in this world," she exclaimed after I finished. "I know you go into your own world now and then, Ona, but who would have thought you had this whole other existence? When did this all start?"

"Ever since Papa died."

"*Hmm, Na wa o!*"

It was clear to me that I had hurt my grandmother by keeping Luenah a secret from her. I had no regrets about not telling her earlier, though. I only wished I had told her under more relaxed circumstances. That would have made it easier to explain how I received those revelations from my grandfather.

"You are such a strange one, Ona," she continued. "I always knew there was something about you, but I couldn't put my finger on it. Anyway, stranger things have happened."

"Grandma, nothing can be stranger than how Okem came into our lives."

"I'm still in shock about that too," my grandmother said, waving her hand. "I also can't believe what you've been through. And to think that you didn't even breathe a word of it to me," she concluded, shaking her head.

"I'm sorry, Grandma. You were so distraught about Papa. You never wanted anyone to bring him up in conversation."

"I was trying to protect you. I knew how close you were to him," she countered.

"I'm so sorry, Ma."

"I'm sorry, too. These past few years must have been excruciating for you. If you had involved me, I would have helped you navigate these issues. You shouldn't have tried to do it all on your own."

"I agree. Sometimes, I wonder why I had to suffer so much to get to where I am right now. I endured Albert while Okem—my number one addiction, my passion, who was carefully sealed and specially delivered to me—languished away in the background."

"Usually, we don't need to look so far beyond ourselves to find the things we want the most," my grandmother intimated.

"I know that now, Mama. My prince was right under my nose all this while, and I was busy searching all over the world trying to find him. Why did I have to kiss a frog to finally get to him? Why?"

I grabbed my stomach to suppress the gag making its way to my throat.

"I should think you would know the answer to that question by now, Ona. Aren't you the one that's been going in and out of this other world?"

"I do actually," I said, grinning mischievously. "If I hadn't kissed the frog, how would I have recognized the taste of my prince when I savored it?"

Her eyes widened, and she cackled.

"You are so right, my dear. It's amazing what one can achieve if they make finding the truth their mission. And don't forget, even though you took the wrong turn when you decided to marry Albert, that move eventually brought you to the right path. In the process, you got all the grooming you needed both on earth and in that other dimension. What did you call it?"

"Luenah!"

I laughed and pinched myself to confirm I wasn't in Luenah. It felt as though my grandfather drove home a point through some sort of telepathic influence. I pictured him smiling and nodding wherever he was.

"Yes, that's it. Nice name."

"You should go there with me sometime."

"No," she snapped. "I think I'll stay right here."

* * *

Still in shock and in need of more avenues to relieve the tension I was feeling, I called Amah after I left my grandmother's room. She had now settled beautifully into her program. I had to cover my ears as her screams when she heard me on the other end of the phone threatened to burst my eardrums.

She screamed even louder after I relayed everything that had happened to me, including the abuse I suffered in Albert's hand.

"Hello, hello," I kept saying to get her attention.

"*Eh*? What?" she continued. "Even with all his money and class, he was hitting you? *Chinekemmee o.* Almighty God."

"Amah, calm down."

"Calm down what?"

"Okay, keep screaming. I hope now you see the

truth in the saying 'not all that glitters is gold.'"

"Hmm, I see that now. But this one is too much. What will happen to Ifedi now? *Chai.*"

"I'll have to turn her over to the authorities."

"I can't believe everything you've gone through. To think I was envious of you this whole time, wanting to be in your shoes."

"My dear, we must all follow our own path. I still am so grateful for where I am today. Count your blessings, and let me count mine."

* * *

My grandmother had wanted to immediately hand Ifedi over to the authorities and let them deal with her, but I convinced her otherwise. After careful thought, I figured it would do no good as Ifedi could deny every bit of the accusation and go scot-free. I thought of a plan to force a confession out of her. If it worked, then I would have absolute proof of her involvement in my grandfather's demise, and if it didn't, then I would be faced with a dilemma. Although I had no doubt my grandfather's revelation was factual, I still battled with what I thought I knew about my impeccable nanny, turned companion.

I waited for everybody to go to sleep. At close to midnight when the only illumination from outside were the street lamps from the homes in the valley, I snuck into my grandfather's bedroom to search for the gourd used to serve his nightly palm wine. I recalled exactly where my grandmother placed it. Many a night, I had helped my grandmother retrieve it from the shelf on the small storage adjoining his bedroom. I prayed Ifedi hadn't discarded it to obliterate evidence of the crime. But so many years had passed. Even if it was still available, any traces of poison may now be undetectable, I thought.

I was elated when I entered the storage room and found the gourd and the drinking bowl my grandfather enjoyed his nightly palm wine with, sitting in its familiar position. I gasped almost too loudly and had to place my hand over my mouth to keep any more sounds from coming out of it. My eyes watered as I stood there for a second staring at the gourd and wondering if I had the strength to reach for it. I finally grabbed it and experienced shockwaves running through my spine. Holding both the gourd and the cup to my chest, I walked into the bedroom and sat on my grandfather's bed for a few minutes, and allowed the tears in my eyes to flow freely down my cheeks as I pondered if my plan would work. Something in my head—my instinct, I believe—told me to go ahead.

I went back to my room and waited until the first morning light. Thinking about everything and what the future might hold for all of us and mostly if the mission I was about to embark on would be successful, robbed me of sleep that night. I needed to be alert, so I could act before Ifedi, who was usually out and about by six got up to start her morning chores. By force of habit, every morning, right before she prepared breakfast for the family, she took a moment and had some bread and tea, all the while whistling the same tune I'd become accustomed to for years.

At five, I snuck into the kitchen and placed the gourd and cup on the small table where she usually ate her bread and tea. I even poured in a little palm wine I found in the fridge before heading to my room and waiting till the clock struck six. Just as I'd expected, I heard Ifedi whistling in the hallway. I counted to thirty before I crept downstairs and proceeded to watch her through the gap in the kitchen door. She opened the fridge and brought out a loaf of bread. With her cup of tea in her hand, she headed to the chair and table in the corner, but she didn't make it halfway through. The teacup dropped on the floor, making a loud crashing sound right before Ifedi fell on her knees with a thud.

"Ifedi!" I screamed, running towards her.

She turned around to look at me. For a moment, terror was written all over her face, and then it was gone, like the sun disappearing into the sea at dusk.

I heard my grandmother scampering down the stairs, and in a flash, she arrived in the kitchen.

"*Ogini*? What is it?" she yelled, panting heavily when she saw Ifedi on her knees and the teacup scattered all over the floor.

Ifedi attempted to rise, but lost her balance and tried again. I stretched out my arm to help her, but she swatted it as though I was a fly and jumped on her feet. Now, her lips were pursed, and her brown eyes stared into the distance. Sweat was running down her forehead.

"It's Ifedi," I said in a triumphant tone as my grandmother continued to stare.

Ifedi glared at me as she adjusted her wrapper, which by now had loosened to expose a fair amount of her heaving breasts. My grandmother looked on in awe and shook her head before turning on her heels. That was when she sighted the gourd.

"What on earth is this doing here?" she said, to no one in particular.

"I...I...don't know," Ifedi muttered.

"Ona," my grandmother called.

"Grandma."

"Who put this here?"

I chuckled, sans humor but refused to answer. My plan had worked more than I could ever have anticipated. I didn't know what was going through Ifedi's head, but I knew what was needed next.

* * *

I, my grandmother, and two older members of our family confronted Ifedi in the dining room at my grandmother's house. One look at her told me she was as guilty as sin.

"Ifedi," I said, facing her squarely. "So, you only came here to destroy this home?"

"I don't know what you're talking about," she said, shifting her gaze from place to place, feigning ignorance.

"Ona, let me handle this," my grandmother demanded. "I need to cut to the chase. There's no time for nonsensical talk right now. Ifedi, do you know what happened to my husband?" she asked Ifedi, who was standing a few feet from her.

"Your husband? No." Ifedi said, grimacing and shrugging her shoulders.

"I don't think you know who you're dealing with," Grandma continued. "I'm going to call the police to arrest you right now if you don't tell the truth. I'm sure they'll be able to beat the truth out of your mouth."

"I-I didn't do anything, Ma."

"You're such a good liar," I said, shaking my head. "Had I not ignored my instincts, I would have figured you out all these years."

"Ifedi, say the truth," my grandmother yelled hysterically. "The truth will set you free. Say the truth!"

Ifedi shifted nervously in her position. My grandmother's reaction had succeeded in getting her to understand the seriousness of her situation.

"I don't know what you're talking about, Ma," she pleaded, dipping her index finger on her tongue before pointing it to the ceiling and swearing she did not know what happened to my grandfather.

"Don't worry, Mama," I said. "The person with the proof that she poisoned Papa's palm wine is bringing it tomorrow. Maybe then, she'll realize this is not a joke and start cooperating."

"What proof," Ifedi asked, her chest heaving intensely up and down.

"Ifedi, stop these denials. Your accomplices ratted out your actions to the authorities," I lied, hoping she would fall for it and confess.

She fell for my fib and realizing the enormity of her situation, with the events from that morning and talk about poison and accomplices, a truth I learned in Luenah, she began to flail her hands and point fingers.

"It's Ozumba and Ekema," she screeched. "I had nothing against your grandfather. They're the ones you should be harassing, not me."

"Did you help Ozumba and Ekema accomplish their mission?" The first elder asked in a calm tone. "I'm asking because you haven't said anything about your involvement. Did you poison the palm wine or not?"

"I can't believe you're listening to this spoilt brat," she said, pointing in my direction. "I have a reputation to protect. What does she have? She goes around town running after two boys like she has no shame. What were you doing in Okem's hotel? Have you no shame?"

I stared with my mouth open as she continued to rain insults on me.

"Shut up!" my grandmother yelled when she couldn't bear it anymore. "Are you mad, Ifedi?"

"I'm not mad, Ma. I was just trying to say—"

"You were trying to say what? Enough! *Anuofia*, wild animal. I don't want to hear *pim* from you again. One more word from you, and I'll give you a dirty slap. Not only did you kill my husband, but you sent Albert after my granddaughter to finish her off. Instead of responding to the allegations, you're pointing fingers at everyone. The worst part is that you stand in front of me, in my own house, and call Ona such awful names, and you say you're not mad."

While my grandmother was yelling at Ifedi, I felt thousands of goosebumps rising on my skin, and a feeling of déjà vu crept all over me. I recalled how Albert had treated me after he turned me into his punching bag. Ifedi's attack was an identical scenario, only, it presented itself in a different situation. My grandfather had told me one time I was in Luenah that the culprit always looks for someone else to blame for their actions. A lot of times, they blame the victim, the one who has suffered the most already, only because they're easy bait.

"It's just a ploy," he said, "to further manipulate the victim and milk them to the very last drop. That is the way of bullies when they're confronted." Thank God for that lesson because I didn't fall for the tactic this time. I pitied Ifedi and wished things could have been different. She had been a wonderful teacher and companion. Who knew she was so evil? All those years living under my grandparent's roof, and we never sniffed her out. She will have to spend the rest of her life in jail, at least that's the penalty for killing a human being here in Ntebe.

CHAPTER TWENTY-TWO

THE POLICE SIREN jolted me out of bed later that afternoon. Through the window, I could see two armed policemen stepping out of their vehicle. My grandmother was running frantically towards them as she wrapped the *ankara* cloth around her chest. I couldn't make out what they were saying, but I knew there was trouble when my grandmother placed both hands over her head, and the policemen rushed past her into the house. I threw on my robe and ran to the living room downstairs to see what was going on.

"She has run away," my grandmother shrieked when she saw me.

"What do you mean she has run away," I asked, just as the policemen returned to the room.

"Mama, we're leaving now," one of the men said with utmost urgency. "We have to search the vicinity before she skips town."

Ifedi had disappeared without a trace from the home we all shared for so many years. My grandmother had asked her to pack her belongings and leave the house after our earlier confrontation. We had expected the police to arrive within minutes to interrogate her, but she beat us to it and absconded before the policemen turned up, while my grandmother and the two elders waited patiently in the sitting room. We couldn't tell if she fled through the window in her room or through an act of magic because the only two valid exits in the home were guarded at the time she made her escape. We later heard that Ozumba had vanished too. Ekema wasn't so lucky. She was captured by officers at the gate of the city as she tried to abscond.

* * *

Ekema's trial was short. They sentenced her to twenty-five years in prison for murder and treason. Right before she was to leave to serve her sentence, Okem confronted her in the prison cell. I insisted on going with him and waited in the shadows as he approached her. She was crouched in a corner chanting obscenities and drawing images on the ground with white chalk. At first, she refused to speak to him, but when she realized he wasn't going anywhere, she stared at him with blood-shot eyes, filled with anger and hatred, and yelled, "Get away from here, you murderer. I don't know who asked you to come here. Go back to where you belong."

"Are you referring to me?" Okem asked, looking around and eventually turning to face her again.

"Yes, you," she continued yelling. "Who else could I have been speaking about? You're an ingrate and a nonentity."

She went on a tirade, cursing and swearing, speaking so fast I couldn't make sense of most of the things that came out of her mouth. Okem, his arms akimbo, stood frowning before his wicked aunt. She continued to berate him, only stopping when she started gasping for breath.

"Look in the mirror and tell me if you don't see a murderer in it," Okem responded. "You stole my childhood, deprived my parents of their offspring while you and Ozumba positioned Albert to take over the kingdom that wasn't his in the first place. To top it all, you murdered Ona's grandfather. I wouldn't be surprised if you caused the demise of my father, too."

The moment she heard mention of the late King, she got up from the ground and faced Okem, her chains rattling as she moved. The blank look that appeared in her eyes reminded me of pure evil. It was the same look I saw in Ifedi's eyes after we confronted her.

Okem must have seen something in it too because he screamed: "Did you kill my father, too?"

The woman hissed.

"I'm serving a life sentence already. I'll be dead before the twenty-five years run out. Isn't that enough for you?"

"Not quite. If I can prove that you murdered my father, I'll add hard labor."

* * *

Before Ekema left to serve her sentence, she confessed Ifedi's role in my grandfather's poisoning. She and Ozumba had promised to take Ifedi to America if she could assist Albert in seizing the throne. In return for her confession, she pleaded for Albert to be spared, claiming he was oblivious of the plot and the activities of the cabal. There wasn't much to spare, though. Albert was fighting for his life. According to his doctor's reports, he drifted in and out of consciousness on a regular basis. Once, I visited him, and in a conscious moment, he attempted to relay a message to me. I could tell that whatever he was trying to say to me was important, but I couldn't make one word out of the buzzing sound coming from his throat. His eyes looked distressed, and he contorted his face as he frantically tried to get across to me. I kept saying, "huh?" and coming closer to get him to calm down and try again. Before I got the chance to ask for a pen and paper for him to write his thoughts down, his doctor whisked me away, claiming I had caused him to relapse and forcing me to promise never to visit him at the hospital again. The latest doctor's report revealed that if he ever made it out alive, he could end up relying on a feeding tube since a vital portion of his oral cavity had been destroyed by the bullet. I felt sorry for him despite the torture he had put me through. He was basically my worst enemy, but I still wished I could save his life.

* * *

The kingmakers approved the annulment of my engagement to Albert. They agreed that a marriage between us was not ordained by the gods. Albert had been unable to pick up the staff before the King died in what they now claimed to be mysterious circumstances. The investigation that was initiated to determine if Ekema and Ozumba had a hand in the King's death progressed smoothly until Albert's testimony was needed to fill in the gaps. A warrant was issued for Ozumba's arrest, and a reward was offered for anyone that could provide valid evidence of his and Ifedi's whereabouts.

* * *

Okem and the kingmakers concluded the staff possession ceremony while hundreds of witnesses waited in the palace grounds. The kingmakers, dressed in their ceremonial attire—red wrappers and long red caps with feathers of differing lengths stuck on the side—marked their faces with chalk in artistic patterns. Whispers filled the air as Okem, in full kingly regalia, entered the sanctuary where the staff was preserved. The witnesses conversed with one another and waited with bated breath for him to emerge with the staff. I had no doubt he would succeed as he'd accomplished that task in Luenah, but no one else in the crowd knew, which explained the anxious looks on their faces as they waited for him to perform. The masses were fed up with the suffering caused by the gap left by the old King and were all eager for Okem to succeed.

Okem took the staff with ease, and emerged from the sanctuary, amidst cheers from all his supporters. He raised the staff for all to see. The kingmakers lined up one after the other to examine it and chanted blessings and adoration for the new King. They formed a tight circle around him and communed with one another, while everyone waited patiently. Ten minutes later, they broke the circle and faced the crowd.

"The road is clear," the Chief Kingmaker announced, to which the other kingmakers, all five of them, chanted, "It is indeed clear."

The gunslingers, strategically positioned outside, fired congratulatory gunshots to announce to the entire kingdom that a new king had been found. The shots continued at fifteen-minute intervals while the coronation ceremony was going on.

The Chief Kingmaker led Okem to the throne and crowned him King of Ide. Each of the kingmakers handed him gifts with varying symbolic meanings in carefully handcrafted boxes. He thanked each of them and placed the gifts on the table beside him.

The last of the kingmakers handed him a book also, and proclaimed: "Take heed to the fourth verse of the twenty-first chapter of the last section."

The *book of life* was considered the most valuable of the gifts he could receive at his coronation. It was said to contain the truth. Anyone who read it and acted according to its precepts would surely become wise. Okem took the book, kissed it, and tucked it under his arm.

He delivered a heartfelt speech and promised that during his rule, he would bring abundance and harmony to the kingdom. He also promised to right all wrongs. The crowd cheered loudly after his speech, and the whole town celebrated for a whole week afterwards.

* * *

Okem reunited with his mother in an emotional ceremony that resulted in a pool of tears on the palace grounds. The Queen, having been deprived of her child since birth, couldn't fathom the amount of wickedness she'd been meted. From then on, Okem doted on her as he tried to make up for a lifetime of separation. She became extremely fond of me, cherishing my role in her son's life. Over dinner at the palace one beautiful evening, she gifted me a vast amount of land and buildings.

"Take it, Ona, my dear," she insisted after I rejected her offer twice. "I owe everything to you, but I'm only offering you a small portion. Whether you accept or not, I'll be placing everything in trust for you to access whenever you're ready."

"No, your highness, the happenings were not my doing. I can't honestly bring myself to receive a reward for something I didn't do."

"What nonsense," the Queen countered. "You restored my son and my entire legacy to me. Consider this my show of gratitude. Besides, you can create bad fortune by rejecting anything that comes freely to you, especially if it can be of benefit to you or others. Doing so," she insisted, "is telling your spirit to withhold further good from coming to you. Is that what you want?"

The Queen made absolute sense, so I didn't need further convincing. This was a lesson I already received during one of my trips to Luenah. Her endowment—estimated to be a quarter of all she owned—turned me into one of the richest women in Ide and Ntebe combined.

* * *

We got married soon after in pomp and style. Our love had endured many difficulties, but we settled into married life with ease. Okem ruled with diligence and wisdom. He was a natural, having practiced for this role since he was born. He gave the late King a befitting burial, one he felt the late Ideme would be proud of wherever he was. With help from a carefully selected cabinet, he was able to turn the economy around and reverse all the damage Ozumba and Ekema had caused when they controlled the affairs of the kingdom. He placed deserving people in positions of power and revived industries. Bribery and corruption seized.

The months of coaching I received to become Albert's Queen came in handy as I assumed my new role with ease. I followed Okem's lead, but I was able to guide him in the right direction when I thought he was making the wrong decision. His regime resulted in an end to the boundary clashes between Ide and Ntebe. He involved the federal government in negotiations to resolve the border disputes and destroy the slums. Properly planned housing projects sprang up in their place. The culprits who orchestrated and benefited from the clashes were tried and punished. A number of them were prestigious members of society. These persons had participated in the original peace talks and purposely created recommendations to benefit their bottom line rather than the wellbeing of the populace. Also implicated were the corrupt judges that handled the past court cases. They were tried and sentenced as well for having received bribes to rule in favor of the cabal.

CHAPTER TWENTY-THREE

I ENTERED LUENAH one more time. In the middle of the afternoon, when the sun was still high in the sky, I was resting on my bed when I slowly drifted away. I walked triumphantly through the path and landed right at the door of the shrine. As I kicked off my shoes, for the first time since my adventures in Luenah began, I noticed a lovely pair of gold slippers glistening on the floor. They felt like a second skin when I tried them on. Heading in the direction of the throne room, my grandfather appeared and led me before the supreme ruler.

"It's time to return the box," the ruler said.

"Which box," I asked, a little confused.

"The one you received in Luenah the day you turned eighteen. Don't tell me you've forgotten about it already."

"Ohh!" I exclaimed.

I had completely forgotten about the box, but right before he asked for it, I had felt something weighing me down, so much so that my right shoulder drooped. *Don't tell me I have been carrying this around all this time.* I reached for my pocket, and there it was, still intact but much heavier than I expected. It was light and empty when I placed it there. Lifting it with both hands, I noticed Papa's amused grin as I panted and heaved from the load.

"Open it," he said.

"Open it?" I muttered under my breath, scared of what I might find inside. It looked like the same box my grandfather handed to me several moons ago, but this one gave me a bad feeling. I shuddered as I alternated my gaze between the intricate designs on the box, the supreme ruler, and my grandfather.

"Go ahead," he repeated. "Open it."

I started to lift the cover slowly and glimpsed

my grandfather looking at me from the corner of his eye. He seemed to be saying, "What is happening, Ona? You've been through this lesson many times."

Mustering all the courage I could find, I opened the box fully and nearly fell over from what came oozing out of it. The hardship I'd endured in the past few years, the disappointments, the pain, the heartbreak, and the turmoil, all flashed before my eyes in streams of light. Each issue with its distinctive color and texture, reminding me of everything I felt, saw, or touched. It took me through the whole realm of all I'd been through. I squirmed at first and then stood stoically as a puzzled look spread across my face.

"Enough," my grandfather said and took the box from me.

He closed it and placed it in his pocket, and turned to me, a contented look on his face.

"What just happened?" I asked, astounded by all I'd seen.

He hesitated for a second before saying. "When you received the box, I bet you thought you were getting a prize."

"Yes. I thought so."

"If you recall, I also told you an exchange was required, right?"

I nodded twice, eager for him to continue.

"Well, remember when you missed the first exchange, I said you would have to give something else in return."

I shrugged.

"I had no clue what you needed me to give, and I still have no clue now."

"I couldn't tell you either what it is you had to give in exchange. It comes as the sum of the actions, the experiences, and the events that occurred in your quest for love and happiness, everything you've experienced. Everything you just saw in that box."

"I see. Why–"

"Shh," he said, placing his index finger on his mouth. "The price was yours to pay. That was the cost of your dreams. The cost of finding and occupying your purpose."

I sighed as I recalled all the pain and disappointment I'd been through.

"But why did I have to bear so much?"

"Everything that happened, the good, the bad, and the ugly, brought you to the point you're at now, and whether you like it or not, brought you closer to your purpose."

"Did it have to involve so much trauma?"

"No, but would you have rather not lived?"

I shook my head furiously.

"Not at all."

He shrugged in triumph as the rest of the court, my fellow *Eris*, who had been staring at me in admiration the whole time I stood there, clapped in unison.

"Everyone is proud of you, Ona. What do you say?"

"Thank you! Thank you!" I said, bowing to the crowd twice with both hands joined together in front of me."

They clapped some more.

"When you were suffering," my grandfather continued after the clapping had died down, "you were in the belly of the whale. That was the time you had to reflect, make supplication, mature, and garner the knowledge needed to understand not only what your purpose was but also how you can occupy it, so you can eventually fulfill it. From now on, you have the responsibility to do everything in your power to stay on course."

"I will, Papa. I will"

I let the things Grandfather said sink in until my thoughts drifted back to Albert, Ozumba, and Ifedi.

"What makes humans act so evil?"

"Simple. They stray so far away from God and leave a gaping hole within their soul that creates a burning need to be filled. This space then gets packed with greed, jealousy, and discontentment, and they're left with no choice but to do wicked deeds. They keep pursuing their dreams, like you and me but end up trampling over others in the process and creating ruin and destruction wherever they go."

I grimaced and shook my head. "What a wicked scary world."

"You have absolutely no reason to be scared," he said, nodding his head.

"Why do you say that?"

He stopped and smiled at me as he used to when I was a little girl.

"Because God is within you! You will not be moved! He will save you from roaming the earth without a purpose!" my grandfather concluded and vanished into thin air.

I returned to earth, the least confused I'd ever been after a trip to Luenah. The rays of the sun poured into the room in full blast shrouding my vision. As I stepped down from the bed to draw the blinds, I saw glistening on my feet the gold slippers I wore at the entrance to the shrine. Confused, I shut my eyes to confirm I had returned to earth. Everything around me—starting from the piercing rays of light, to the mango trees outside, and the birds on the windowsill—confirmed my exact location. As I pondered what to make of the shoes, my ears perked at the sound of a sweet booming voice, saying, "You're now ready to occupy your purpose."

THE END

Acknowledgments

First, I would like to thank the Almighty God, the source of my inspiration and without whom everything would be nothing.

Writing a novel is a very lonely exercise, so when I emerge from my cocoon, I feel blessed to be surrounded by people I admire.

Massive love and appreciation for my favorite trio, Ofor, Dumkele, and Nnamdi. Nnamdi, for being my first reader and a frank one at that. Dumkele, for completing detailed and comprehensive edits. Ofor, for creating my digital productions and handling behind the scenes marketing.

To my beta readers Ogbo, Kene, Azubuike, Urunna, and Ogo, I greatly appreciate you giving me the gift of your time to read my drafts. Your advice and feedback really helped me take the story to new levels. To Urunna, thank you for bringing my idea of the box to life.

To my publicists, virtual assistants, and graphic designers, thank you for your help and guidance through this daunting process. I can't imagine how I would have coped without your help.

A big thanks to my family and friends. You have been there from the beginning, supporting and encouraging me.

Finally, a huge thank-you to my readers. You make me feel that the massive effort involved in writing and publishing a book is worth its while.

ABOUT THE AUTHOR

Oby Aligwekwe is the author of Nfudu and Hazel House. The Place Beyond Her Dreams is her Young Adult debut. A talented writer, Oby is also an inspirational speaker and a chartered accountant. She lives in Oakville, Ontario with her family and supports her community through her charity Éclat Beginnings.

Twitter: @obyaligwekwe
Facebook: obyaligwekweauthor
Instagram: obyaligwekwe
www.obyaligwekwe.com

ALSO BY

OBY ALIGWEKWE

Praise for NFUDU

"A Delicious Read" – KC M, London, UK

"A Heart Tugging Story" – Juliet, Canada

"Very educative, with lots of history interwoven with romance, and filled with suspense and crazy twists that took my breath away." – Chikaego, U.S

ALSO BY

OBY ALIGWEKWE

Praise for Hazel House

"Nail-biting suspense with twists and turns, not knowing whodunnit until the very end." – Lena, Canada

"A must read for lovers of murder mysteries and romance, with enough suspense, intrigues, twists and turns to keep you on the edge to the very last page." – Ifey, US